"What's on the paper?"

A flash of panic shot through her eyes. "What paper?"

"The one I overheard you mention. Where did it come from?"

Several seconds passed in silence. Finally Allison sighed. "The newel post in my house. I found it after the break-in. All it had on it was numbers and letters."

"Any idea what they mean?"

"Not a clue."

For the next several moments she didn't meet his eyes. Blake was pretty sure she was telling the truth. But he was equally sure there was something she was keeping from him. He had to make her trust him.

"Not to scare you or anything, but what do you think this guy is going to do when he exhausts places to search? What do you think his next step will be?"

She slowly lifted her gaze and met his. Her eyes were filled with fear. "I have no idea. I try not to think about it. Because if I did, I'd never sleep again."

Books by Carol J. Post

Love Inspired Suspense

Midnight Shadows
Motive for Murder
Out for Justice
Shattered Haven

CAROL J. POST

From medical secretary to court reporter to property manager to owner of a special events decorating company, Carol's résumé reads like someone who doesn't know what she wants to be when she grows up. But one thing that has remained constant through the years is her love for writing. She started as a child, writing poetry for family and friends, then graduated to articles, which actually made it into some religious and children's publications. Several years ago (more than she's willing to admit), she penned her first novel. In 2010, she decided to get serious about writing fiction for publication and joined Romance Writers of America, Tampa Area Romance Authors and Faith, Hope & Love, RWA's online inspirational chapter. She has placed in numerous writing contests, including RWA's 2012 Golden Heart®.

Carol lives in sunshiny central Florida with her husband (who is her own real-life hero) and writes her stories under the shade of the oaks in her yard. She holds a bachelor's degree in business and professional leadership, which doesn't contribute much to writing fiction but helps a whole lot in the business end of things. Besides writing, she works alongside her music minister husband singing and playing the piano. She also enjoys sailing, hiking, camping—almost anything outdoors. Her two grown daughters and grandson live too far away for her liking, so she now pours all that nurturing into taking care of three fat and sassy cats and one highly spoiled dog.

SHATTERED HAVEN

CAROL J. POST

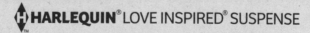HARLEQUIN® LOVE INSPIRED® SUSPENSE

Recycling programs
for this product may
not exist in your area.

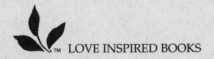 LOVE INSPIRED BOOKS

ISBN-13: 978-0-373-04240-1

Shattered Haven

www.Harlequin.com

Printed in U.S.A.

Come to Me, all you who labor and are heavy laden, and I will give you rest. Take My yoke upon you and learn from Me, for I am gentle and lowly in heart, and you will find rest for your souls
For My yoke is easy and My burden is light.
—*Matthew* 11:28–30

First of all, I would like to thank
all the wonderful people in Cedar Key
who patiently answered my questions—
Chief Virgil Sandlin of the Cedar Key Police
Department, Chief Robert Robinson of the
Cedar Key Fire Department, Debbie Smith
of the Cedar Key Chamber of Commerce,
Leslie Landress of the Harbour Master Suites
and too many others to list.
You've made researching this book a joy.

Thank you to my family for your encouragement
and support and talking me up to all your friends.

To my critique partners, Karen Fleming,
Dixie Taylor and Sabrina Jarema,
for your valuable input and the great plotting
and research weekends in Cedar Key.
We managed to have lots of fun amid all the work.

To my awesome editor, Rachel Burkot,
and my wonderful agent, Nalini Akolekar.
You're both the greatest!

And thank you to my husband, Chris.
If I had it to do all over again, I'd still choose you.

ONE

Allison Winchester lay stock-still, every muscle tight with apprehension.

Something had awoken her. A noise. Different from the usual creaks and groans of the old Victorian.

But all was quiet. Was it her imagination? The remnants of a dream?

She eased into a semi-upright position and propped herself on her elbows. A full moon cast its silver glow into the room, the lace curtains making shadowed patterns on the furnishings. The door was closed, her robe hanging from a hook on its back. Next to the bed, two shams and a half dozen throw pillows lay stacked in the upholstered chair with a stuffed Garfield perched on top. Everything was exactly as she had left it. A sliver of tension slid away.

Then it came again. A rattle. Like someone trying to jimmy a window. The tension ratcheted up again, and she lay frozen, ears straining in the silence that followed. When the rattle resumed, she had no doubt. Someone was trying to break into her house.

She sprang from the bed and snatched her cell phone from her purse. As she finished punching in the three numbers, the crash of breaking glass shattered the still night. Panic raced up her spine and settled in her chest, squeezing the air from her lungs. Disjointed prayers circled through her mind, along with frantic commands—lock the door, hide, grab Tom's gun. When she was finally able to breathe again, her ragged gasp echoed in the spacious room.

Then another sound registered—a calm female voice.

"Nine-one-one. What is your emergency?"

"Someone's in my house." Her voice was a raspy whisper.

The dispatcher continued her soothing tone. "Help is on the way. I'm staying on the line until they arrive."

Allison tiptoed to the door and silently turned the lock. Downstairs, heavy footsteps thudded against the polished hardwood floors. Her intruder wasn't even trying to be quiet. She clutched the phone more tightly and pressed it against her ear, that soothing voice her lifeline to safety.

The footsteps hesitated, and for several moments, she forgot to breathe. Then a new noise shattered her already frayed nerves— the creak of the bottom step. Renewed panic spiraled through her. *Lord, please help me.*

"He's coming upstairs." Where were the police? What was taking them so long?

She drew in a shaky breath. Probably less than a minute had passed since she had first placed her call. But she wasn't going to wait helplessly while a possible killer made his way toward her room.

She backed away, eyes still glued to the door. If he wanted to come in, the lock wouldn't stop him. One solid kick, and the door frame would splinter. She propped the phone against her ear with one shoulder and opened her T-shirt drawer, cringing at the scrape of wood on wood. There hadn't been any more creaks. Maybe he had abandoned his plans for coming upstairs. But she wasn't taking a chance.

Her fingers scrabbled along the bottom of the drawer, reaching for what had lain untouched since she moved to Cedar Key two years ago. When her hand made contact with cold steel, trepidation warred with relief. Holding something so lethal just didn't feel...safe. She had outgrown her youthful klutziness. But she still didn't feel confident handling a weapon.

Now wasn't the time for such reservations.

"I'm getting my gun." She kept her voice low.

"Help is on the way. Just stay put."

"Believe me, I will." No way was she leaving the room. At least until the cops arrived and the intruder was cuffed.

She propped the phone against her shoulder and inserted the loaded clip, hands shaking. Then she waited, weapon trained on the door, her finger poised on the trigger.

According to Tom, the pink Glock was a

perfect ladies' gun. He'd bought it for her a month before he was killed, insisting she keep it with her. He'd even tried to teach her how to use it.

She should have paid more attention. But she hadn't seen the need. She lived in an upper-class New England neighborhood, separated from the unsavory elements of society. And blind to the unscrupulous activities of her husband. Those same activities had left her a widow at age twenty-four. Tom had needed the gun worse than she had.

A siren sounded in the distance and screamed closer. Her breath spilled out in a relieved sigh. "They're almost here."

She moved to the side window and looked out over the small yard that lay along the west side of her house. She wouldn't be able to see the police. But the reflection of flashing lights in the window of her neighbor's bungalow would signal their arrival.

A second later, the siren stopped. A figure appeared from the back and charged across her side yard at a full run. Within moments, he had disappeared behind the hedge bordering her neighbor's backyard.

She laid the weapon on the dresser, disconnected the call and grabbed her robe from the back of the door. The intruder was probably long gone, but she needed to tell the police what she saw. She hurried down the stairs, then crossed the small foyer.

As soon as she stepped onto her front porch, she stopped short. A Cedar Key police cruiser sat in her front yard. But the officer wasn't alone. He had already apprehended the suspect. He had him pinned against the side of the car and was cuffing him.

She cinched the belt on her robe more tightly and started down the porch steps. The officer turned and nodded a greeting. It was Hunter Kingston. He had somehow managed to catch the intruder and drag him back to the cruiser before she could get down the stairs and out the door. Hunter was good, but she didn't know he was *that* good.

He looked her up and down. "Are you all right?

"Yeah, I'm fine. He didn't come upstairs.

I'm guessing your siren scared him away."
She cast a glance at the suspect. "You can bet
I won't forget to set the alarm again."

One edge of Hunter's mouth turned up.
He obviously recognized her comment for
what it was — a threat to the intruder. She had
never considered installing an alarm system,
had never felt the need.

The stranger turned when she spoke. In
the glow of the nearby streetlight, he was
an imposing figure, even with his hands
secured behind his back. A Guy Harvey
T-shirt stretched taut over a muscular chest,
and massive arms spoke of hours in the gym.
With the close-cut hair, firm set of his jaw
and sense of authority he exuded, he didn't
fit the image of a common burglar. He looked
more like a military guy. Or a cop.

His eyes shifted from her back to Hunter.
"What's going on?"

"Someone broke into this lady's house."

"It wasn't me. I already told you, I was
chasing my dog."

His tone was nonchalant, the concern she
would expect to see absent. Either he had

a lot of confidence in his ability to talk his way out of trouble, or he had been through enough arrests that the thought of spending some time in jail didn't faze him.

Hunter didn't appear to be buying his story. "At four a.m.?"

"Since three thirty, actually. He saw a cat and took off. I've chased him all over this side of Cedar Key."

"Where are you staying?"

"Cedar Cove Marina, on my boat. I just arrived this afternoon."

"I'm going to have to bring you in for questioning." Hunter opened the back door of the cruiser and guided him around it.

Now the stranger's eyes did fill with concern. "I need to find my dog. He's a young Doberman, answers to Brinks. He won't hurt anybody, but he's probably halfway to the mainland by now."

"We'll keep an eye out for him." Skepticism filled Hunter's tone.

Allison pursed her lips. Something wasn't right about the whole scenario. Hunter would have to be Flash to have covered that much ground by the time she made it outside. She couldn't identify the intruder. Between the clouds obscuring the moon, the oak that shaded a good portion of her side yard and the distance from the streetlight, it was too dark.

But she knew where he had come from and which direction he had gone.

"Hunter, wait." She held up a hand. "Where was he when you saw him?"

"I was coming down First Street, and he ran out from between your house and the one next door." As Hunter spoke, he gestured with his right hand, tracing the path the suspect had taken.

It was all wrong. The intruder came from the opposite side of the house and went in a different direction. The stranger was telling the truth. And for some unexplained reason, she was glad.

"Hunter, we've got the wrong guy."

His brows lifted in question, and she continued.

"I saw the intruder, just as you got here. He ran out from behind my house and went that way." She lifted a hand, her index finger extended.

Before Hunter could respond, a Doberman came bounding toward them and skidded to a stop at the open door of the car. The dog put both front paws in the man's lap and slathered slobbery kisses up one cheek, initiating peals of laughter.

"Now you decide to show up. You almost got me arrested." Still laughing, he maneuvered to his feet. Not easy with two large paws in his lap and his hands cuffed behind his back. "No more jerky treats for you. At least till tomorrow."

Hunter stepped behind him and inserted a key into the handcuffs. "Sorry about that. We don't get many break-ins here. In fact, we don't get *any* break-ins. You were in the wrong place at the wrong time."

The stranger shot him a forgiving smile over one shoulder as the cuffs clicked open. "No problem. You were only doing your job. But I have to admit, this was my first time on this side of the handcuffs." He clipped a leash onto the dog's collar before extending his hand. "Blake Townsend, Dallas PD."

Hunter's brows shot up again. "You've got to be kidding. I was arresting a cop?"

"Former cop, actually. Injured on the job." He turned toward Allison. "And you, milady, deserve a big thank-you for getting me out of hot water. I at least owe you dinner."

The smile he gave her reached his eyes, creating fine lines at their corners. His manner was joking, but something told her he was dead serious about dinner. And she was suddenly hit with a case of teenage shyness. She reached to smooth her hair, then dropped her hand. Why bother? The first impression was already made—barefoot and bedhead. Not that it mattered.

She returned his smile with one that she hoped projected confidence. "That won't be necessary. Your words were thank-you enough."

He nodded, then looked at Hunter. "If you're done with me, I'll get Bozo here back to the boat. Next time you see us, he'll be on a leash." He frowned down at the dog who eyed him eagerly, tail nub wagging. One ear stood at attention, straight and sharp. The other made an attempt. But the top two inches flopped forward. The imperfection lent a comic element to his would-be ferociousness. "I think he needs obedience training. He's usually a good dog, but when he sees a cat, his brain shuts down and he morphs into seventy pounds of pure, dumb instinct."

He turned and started down the sidewalk, favoring his right leg. Probably the injury he'd mentioned. There was stiffness in his gait, as if he was trying hard to hide what should have been a pronounced limp after spending the last half hour chasing his dog.

A cop. She had him pegged right. Maybe she was getting better at reading people. It was about time.

When she returned her gaze to Hunter, he was grinning at her. "Checking out the newest Cedar Key resident?"

"Not like you're thinking." Her cheeks warmed in spite of her flippant response. Hunter was a good friend. They had a lot in common, right down to their determination to avoid serious relationships with the opposite sex. She didn't know his reasons, but she knew her own. Serious relationships required trust, something in short supply lately, at least on her end.

"Let's check out your place." Hunter's words cut across her thoughts. "We've got a breaking and entering to investigate."

She squared her shoulders and started up the front walk, uneasiness descending on her with every step. Meeting the injured cop had been a nice reprieve. Now she had to face what she would find inside—a broken window, the possibility of items missing from her house.

And the end of the sense of security she had always known there.

Blake picked up a fifty-pound dumbbell and took a seat. The only gym on Cedar Key, Cedar Cove Fitness was well maintained and had everything he needed. And it was within walking distance of his boat. Of course, everything in Cedar Key was within walking distance of his boat.

After finishing his last set, he took a long swig from his water bottle. Tomorrow's workout would be legs, a thought that brought a vague sense of dread. Recent months had given new meaning to the phrase No Pain, No Gain. He ran his hand over the five-inch scar that traveled from his lower thigh down to the top of his shin. All through rehab, he had maintained his upper-body workouts, so that part of his physique hadn't suffered. Unfortunately, he couldn't say the same for his legs.

He slung his towel over his shoulder and moved toward the door. It was time for Brinks's late-afternoon walk. The dog had been cooped up alone on the boat for the past two hours and was probably about stir crazy. But he wasn't going out without a leash. Blake had learned his lesson. Good thing the lady had spoken up last night. Otherwise he might be cooling his heels in the Levy County Jail.

When he stepped onto the dock and approached his boat, a black-and-tan face appeared at one of the windows, and excited barking commenced. Maybe they could take a route that led past the lady's house. He really wanted to check on her. After last night's scare, she had looked so vulnerable, clad in her ankle-length robe, feet bare and hair mussed from sleeping. But what had really gotten to him was the fear that lingered in her eyes. It had made his protective instincts kick into overdrive.

He might catch her outside. If not, from what he had seen during his short time in Cedar Key, people were friendly. A knock on the door from a concerned resident likely wouldn't seem inappropriate or creepy.

As he stepped onto his boat, his gaze drifted to the slips to his right, where a sleek white sailboat was moored. It was there when he arrived yesterday, but had disappeared by the time he returned from lunch. Now it was back, its captain still aboard. She stood in profile, holding a hose. A cone-shaped spray burst from its end, and she worked her way toward the bow with slow side-to-side motions. Once he got Brinks, maybe he would introduce himself.

When he stepped back off his boat, she had

finished her spraying and was walking toward the cockpit, hose still in her hand. He moved closer, the raucous calls of seagulls accompanying his steps. Waves lapped against the pilings, and a gentle breeze rustled his clothes.

He waited to speak until she had stepped down onto the cockpit seat. "Good afternoon, sailor."

She started and spun to face him, a sudden spray of water barely missing his feet. The fear in her eyes instantly turned to relief, and his own widened in surprise. Her blond hair was combed into a thick braid, and a Cedar Key boating hat cast her face in shadow, but he recognized her immediately. She was the same woman who had had the break-in.

"Sorry. I didn't mean to startle you. I was coming over to introduce myself, but we've already met." Sort of. He still didn't know her name.

She laid the hose on the deck and wiped her hand on her shorts before extending it. "We've met but haven't been formally introduced. Allison Winchester."

"Blake Townsend." Of course, she already knew that. "And this is Brinks."

"Like the security company?"

"Yeah, except in his case it's more tongue-in-cheek. He'll lick you to death."

She laughed and extended her arm, palm down. After a quick sniff, Brinks slid his nose under her hand and gave a couple of pushes, encouraging a pat on the head. She complied with some much-loved scratching behind the ears.

"Have they figured out who broke into your house?"

"No, they haven't." She stepped back and began coiling lines and laying them neatly on the deck. "He broke a pane out of one of the library windows, turned the latch and came in that way. Hunter lifted prints, so we'll see what comes back."

"Did he take anything?"

"Not that I can tell. I think he got scared off. My car's in the shop getting a new timing belt, so it wasn't in its usual spot. He probably thought no one was home. He wasn't even trying to be quiet."

Blake leaned against one of the pilings and watched her while she worked. There was something about her that intrigued him. She was definitely pretty. She wore a button-up shirt, its tails tied in a loose knot at her waist, and shorts that stopped a little lower than midthigh. She was lithe and athletic, and even though it was late October, her skin still held a healthy golden glow from summer days spent in the sun.

But it wasn't just her looks that sparked his interest. She possessed a down-to-earth sweetness that sucked him in. Moving about her boat and securing it for the night, she seemed so capable and sure of herself. But he couldn't forget the fear he'd seen in her eyes in the early-morning hours. Or how on edge she'd been when he called out his greeting.

"Are you all right?"

Her eyes met his, and something flickered there, a brief flash of vulnerability. Then she resumed her work zipping the cover over the mainsail.

"Sure. Why?"

"Having your house broken into can be

scary. If there's anything I can do, you know where to find me."

The smile she gave him lit her eyes. "Thanks." She stepped onto the dock and checked the lines she had tied off previously, then straightened. "That's it. Till tomorrow anyway."

"Do you go out every day?" As toned as she was, he wouldn't be surprised.

"Not *every* day. Depends on if I've got charters."

She started down the dock, and he fell in beside her, trying not to favor his right leg. Brinks walked ahead of them, straining at the leash, eager for his walk.

"So you're a charter captain."

"Yep. Mostly morning or afternoon excursions, with some day trips and the occasional multiday thrown in. If I do an overnight, I bring along a cook and crew mate. It's a pretty enjoyable way to make a living."

"That does sound like fun." He scanned the parking area. "I assume your car's still in the shop?"

"Yeah, but I usually walk anyway. It's good exercise."

"Do you mind if we walk with you? I'm past due for his afternoon jaunt, and he's so excited, he can hardly stand it." He nodded down at Brinks. His breathing was strained, restricted by the pressure he was putting on the collar. The crazy dog was half choking himself.

"Sure." She glanced over at him. "Are you vacationing or here for an extended time?"

"Extended." Although how extended was anybody's guess.

"You said you're a cop."

They turned onto Dock Street, where an eclectic array of wooden buildings lined the water's edge. Ahead, a series of bright blue stairs and landings led to Steamers Bar and Grill.

"I *was* a cop. Not anymore."

"Do you think you'll go back to it once your leg heals?"

So she *had* noticed. Either she was really observant, or he wasn't as good at hiding the limp as he had thought. The total knee replacement was a success. The work on the thigh was another story. Reconstructing mincemeat was a bit more challenging.

He shook his head. "Too much permanent damage. I've got to be able to run as fast as the bad guys. This has slowed me down. I took seven hits."

She flinched and offered him a sympathetic smile. "I'm sorry to hear that. So what happened? Did you get caught in a shoot-out?"

"Something like that. I was working undercover. A drug buy went bad."

Of course, there was more to it than that. But he wasn't going to talk about it. Because if he didn't talk about it, he would eventually quit thinking about it. Then maybe the nightmares would stop.

"They offered me a desk job, but I'm not a sit-at-a-desk kind of guy."

She studied him. "I can see that. You seem the type that goes for the action. So what do you do, now that you're not a cop anymore?"

"I'm still figuring that out. I went for my degree in criminal justice right after high school, and I've been a cop ever since. Thought I'd die a cop." Almost did.

"So you're in transition."

"You could say that."

"That's okay, as long as you don't stay there forever."

She was right. And he wouldn't. He had always been too driven to sit idle for long. Besides, eventually the insurance money would run out. But long before then, he'd have his head back on straight and be ready to resume the life he had left in Dallas. With a few adjustments.

They rounded the corner, and Allison's eyes dipped to Brinks. "How often do you have to walk him?"

"Usually four times—when we get up, lunchtime, late afternoon and right before bed. Except this morning. For some reason, he decided at three thirty that he had to go out. Wouldn't leave me alone. We went up on deck, and before I could get his leash on him, he saw the cat and bolted."

"Brinks needs to work on his timing. A

minute earlier, and you might have been in time to catch the bad guy."

When they reached her driveway, she turned to face him. "Thanks for walking with me. I enjoyed your company."

She was smiling, but something had changed. Her posture had stiffened, and her blue eyes had darkened with worry.

He looked past her to the colorful Victorian surrounded by a manicured yard. A polished oak door with stained-glass panels complemented the warm exterior. But inside, the house was cold and empty and silent. And she was walking in alone.

"Would you like me to go in with you? You know, check the windows and doors?"

She hesitated while indecision flashed across her features. Finally, she squared her shoulders and mustered a half smile. "That's all right. I don't think he'll be back."

"You sure? I don't mind." He drew his brows together as another thought crossed his mind. "The window's been fixed, right?"

"Terrance did it this morning."

"Terrance?"

"The kid at the marina. Stays on the Bay-liner. He does odd jobs for people around town. You've probably met him."

Yeah, he had. He was quiet and tattooed and walked around with a bit of a chip on his shoulder. Blake didn't know his past, but he had run up against his kind often enough to recognize what was behind that tough-guy facade—a lost kid, trying to prove he could make it without anybody's help.

Blake watched Allison let herself into the house, then continued down the road. He hoped to see more of her. She was a fellow boater. Someone who loved the water as much as he did. And she was just an all-around nice person. He wasn't looking for a romantic relationship, but if something developed, he wouldn't be opposed. As long as it stayed casual.

Keep It Casual—that had been his lifelong motto. Except once. And he was still kicking himself.

Eighteen months ago, both his personal and professional lives took a nosedive. No, they did more than take a nosedive. They crashed and burned. And he'd been trying ever since to regain his equilibrium.

And all the while, Cedar Key beckoned. He had spent a week there every summer for five straight years. That was when he was a kid, and they were still a complete family—him, his mom, his dad and his little sister. Life was perfect then. His police detective dad was good at shielding them from the ugliness he saw every day.

Of all the memories he had of his father, vacations in Cedar Key were some of the best. So last week, he closed up his apartment in Dallas, loaded Brinks into his Explorer, hooked up the boat and made the trip to Galveston. While a friend drove the truck and trailer back home, he headed for Florida. Now he was in paradise, surrounded by the rolling sea, quiet sunsets, quaint shops and friendly people. Hopefully the laid-back atmosphere of Cedar Key would offer the peace and direction that had been missing from his life.

Because if he didn't find it here...well, he just didn't know where else to look.

TWO

Allison laid the book across her lap and looked at the clock hanging on the rose-hued wall. It was ten thirty. A half hour past her usual bedtime. She heaved a sigh. She was stalling, and she knew it.

Last night's break-in had rattled her more than she wanted to admit. During the day, she had done well. First thing this morning, she'd called Terrance and he'd come right out to measure the window and make a list of what he needed. By eleven, the work was done—a new piece of glass installed and paint touched up where the intruder had tried to pry open the window.

The afternoon hadn't been bad, either. With a charter that included three active young boys, she had had plenty to occupy her thoughts. But once her customers had headed back to their vacation cottage, all the distractions were gone. That was when the uneasiness started. She began to tackle her chores, and memories of the prior night surged forward. As the sun sank lower in the sky and darkness became an imminent threat, her tension mounted. Then Blake had called out his booming greeting six feet behind her, almost sending her into cardiac arrest.

But the walk home had been nice. There was something reassuring about having him next to her, Brinks in front. When he offered to go in first, she almost accepted his offer. Then she changed her mind. It was one random break-in. She would buck up and deal with it. She had certainly been through worse.

Learning that Tom had been murdered had knocked the foundation right out from under her. But his death had been just the beginning. Three nights later, two thugs had showed up—the kind of men who broke legs and threw people in the river in concrete boots. They'd been there to make sure she didn't talk. But one couldn't tell what one didn't know. Apparently, they'd believed her, because they'd left her alone after that.

Over the next two months, her life slowly unraveled. The more the authorities delved into Tom's death, the more they learned about his life. And it didn't coincide at all with what she knew. Her Tom was a detective, honest and hardworking. He even moonlighted as a security guard for one of the wealthy Providence families. The Tom the investigation uncovered was a dirty cop owned by the mob. The honorable man she thought she had married didn't exist.

No, after all she went through two and a half years ago, she wouldn't let anything steal the peace she had found on Cedar Key. She pushed herself up from the couch and bent to turn off the lamp. With Blake at her side, shaking off the effects of the break-in had been easy. Now, in the dark, while most of the neighborhood slept, it was a little more difficult.

Maybe she should get a dog. A dog would alert her if someone tried to come into the house. And a deep, threatening growl would likely stop an intruder before he even got that far. Yeah, and what would she do with a dog while she was on the boat? A lot of customers would have a problem with a canine guest.

Maybe an alarm. An alarm wouldn't have to be taken out and walked. It wouldn't eat much, either.

She sighed and started up the stairs, resting her hand against the bronze angel that stood poised atop the newel post. The angel had been there when she bought the house, and although she had completely renovated the old Victorian, it had remained a permanent fixture. Bronze eyes stared straight ahead, serene but alert, as if watching over the house, guarding the front door.

Except now she wasn't facing the door straight on, more like she was guarding the sidelight. Had the angel always been slightly turned? Why hadn't she noticed?

She cupped its back, slipping her fingers between the bronze wings. The chill that had passed over her the night of the break-in crept along her skin again. Did her intruder try to remove the angel from the newel post? No.

With all the valuables in the house, and her iPad and laptop in plain view, the intruder wasn't likely after a bronze finial.

She dismissed the thought and tried to straighten the angel, not really expecting it to move. It did. She twisted it back and forth, pulling upward. The angel didn't come off, but the tugging was creating a small gap in the seam between the top of the post and its sides. Was it supposed to come apart?

She strode to the kitchen and returned with a table knife, then worked her way along the seam on all four sides. The top wasn't nailed to the post. In fact, there didn't seem to be anything holding the two pieces together except countless coats of varnish and decades of swelling in Florida's relentless humidity. She continued to pry, her pulse racing as the gap widened.

Finally the top came loose from the post. She turned it over, checking the underside. A bolt ran through the wood and into the finial, holding the two pieces together. When her gaze moved to the newel post, anticipation coursed through her. It was hollow, its interior hidden in shadow.

She hurried to the foyer closet to retrieve a flashlight, her heart pounding in earnest. Was something of value hidden inside the secret compartment? Was that what her intruder was after?

When she returned to the staircase, she shined the light into the opening. About eight inches down was a thick roll of yellowed paper about two and a half feet long, judging from the height of the post. Blueprint size. She slid it out and began to uncoil it. Just what she suspected—house plans.

Without fully unrolling them, she laid them aside, and they curled back into the shape they had maintained for the past hundred years.

Surely the secret compartment held something more interesting than house plans. But when she shined the light into the opening again, the beam revealed smooth, hard wood, all the way to the bottom. The compartment was empty.

She sank to the bottom step and rested her

chin in her hands, elbows propped against her knees. Maybe her intruder wasn't trying to get into the newel post.

Then why had he tampered with the finial? It hadn't been turned accidentally. All the times she had gone up and down those steps, the angel had never moved.

No, he had broken into the house with plans to retrieve something from that secret compartment. He just hadn't anticipated her being there and the police arriving before he could remove the top.

Which meant he would be back.

The uneasiness she had struggled to keep at bay for the past twenty hours intensified, and she cast a worried glance at the front door. It was locked. So were all the windows. She had checked.

Of course, everything had been locked up last night, too. And that hadn't stopped him.

Well, if he did come back, he would be disappointed...unless he had a fascination with old house plans. She frowned at the thick roll of yellowed papers lying on the hardwood floor. They were an interesting find.

She would have appreciated them under other circumstances. Now she just wanted to know why someone had broken into her house, and a set of ancient house plans wasn't doing anything to help her figure that out.

She knelt next to them and unrolled them fully to find the bound edge, planning to roll them more tightly. She may as well put them back where she found them. But as soon as she reached the inside edge, a smaller page sprang loose from the bound ones.

It was a single sheet, eight and a half by eleven, unlined. Like copy paper. Except it was old. Or maybe it had just gotten wet. The page was crinkled and unevenly yellow. Three lines had been scrawled across the front—each beginning with a letter followed by a series of numbers. Whatever it meant, it probably had nothing to do with the house.

The old Victorian had been in her family for most of the past seventy years. It had gone from her grandparents to her aunt to her cousin. Then to the investor who snapped it up from the courthouse steps five years ago, after her cousin stopped paying the property taxes. He had probably planned to hold on to it until the housing market turned around. But Allison's cash offer persuaded him to change his mind.

So who did the paper belong to? It wasn't the investor. According to the neighbors, he had bought the house, then let it sit empty. Which meant her family had put it there. What did they have that they didn't want anyone to know about? Money? Gold? Pirate treasure?

Yeah, right. Cedar Key had never been a pirate hideout. Besides, if her grandparents had happened onto anything like that, there would be stories. Small towns were known for their gossip. Cedar Key was no different. Of all the tales about her grandparents that circulated around town, not one gave any hint of hidden treasure.

Allison pushed herself to her feet and strode toward the kitchen. What if the numbers were clues to an unsolved crime, a way for her grandparents to get a bad deed off their consciences before they died? What if she solved the puzzle and found a body?

No, her grandparents were a little odd—okay, from the stories her parents told, they were certifiably nuts—but they weren't killers.

Of course, she didn't have firsthand knowledge. Ties had been pretty much severed between her parents and her dad's side of the family long before she was born. Her dad had gone to law school instead of taking over the Winchester clamming business, and his parents never forgave him. Then marrying a New Englander sealed his fate.

On two occasions, her parents had tried to mend the rift between the elder and younger Winchesters and made the trip to Cedar Key. The rift-mending excursions were a total failure. But on those two brief trips, Allison fell in love with the place. When her life in Providence unraveled, Cedar Key seemed the perfect location to start over.

She flipped the switch on her way into the kitchen and flattened the paper against the butcher block island. Light poured from the four inverted globes of the Albany chandelier.

But the random letters and numbers didn't make any more sense there than they had in the dimness of the foyer.

She squinted at the characters scrawled across the page. They were written with a heavy hand, and judging from the sloppiness, jotted down in a hurry:

R45 87

G45 165

R2.55 282

It looked to be some kind of code. But for what? The numbers weren't coordinates. The forty-fifth parallel ran across the northern states, and neither latitude nor longitude went as high as 282.

She stared at the page, trying to think outside the box. But the harder she focused, the more she drew a blank. Maybe after a good night's sleep, the answer would come. If not, she would keep working on it.

As odd as her grandparents had been, they were well liked on Cedar Key. And since Allison had taken back her maiden name and was once again a Winchester herself, it had given her an instant "in." People still spoke fondly of her grandparents, even though they had been gone for years. But maybe they had harbored some secrets. Maybe there were skeletons in the Winchester closet.

Whatever it was, someone apparently knew. If there was something of value that belonged to her family, no outsider was going to take it away from her.

And then there was the other possibility, that the clues would lead to some kind of contraband...or worse. A knot of dread settled in her stomach. The news would travel fast, from one end of Cedar Key to the other. She knew how it worked. She had experienced it all—the sideways glances, the hushed conversations that came to an abrupt halt, the people suddenly too busy for her, people she had thought were her friends.

She folded the paper and slid it into her purse. She needed to find a better hiding place. Contraband or treasure, someone had apparently found out and come to claim it.

Well, he could look all he wanted. She had the clues. And she was determined to get to it first.

* * *

Blake sat on the deck of his Sea Ray, a glass of green tea in one hand and a Sharpie in the other, the latest issue of the *Cedar Key Beacon* open on his lap. Brinks lay stretched out in the sunshine, attached to a spare dock line. In another hour, it would be time to walk him again. Maybe by then Allison would be back, and he could combine the dog's afternoon walk with her trip home. Brinks was great company, but conversation was a little lacking.

Early that morning, he had gone fishing and caught his dinner for the next few evenings. At least, the protein portion of it. Then he had walked Brinks and gone to the gym. After that was a call to his mom. He had already been the cause of enough sleepless nights. He didn't want to compound her worries by not staying in touch.

He drew in a deep breath and leaned back in the seat. Eventually, boredom was going to set in. Even back home, with physical therapy and vocational rehab and the teaching certification classes the work comp carrier had put him through, there was still too much downtime, not enough activity to work off the energy coiled inside. Tough sessions at the gym helped. But they weren't the same as rock climbing with his buddies. Or zigzagging down Vail's black-diamond slopes.

He looked up from his reading to scan the horizon. Two sailboats cut through the waves, but neither were Allison's. When he turned back toward Cedar Cove Beach and Yacht Club, the kid he had met yesterday was making his way down the dock in flip-flops, an Old Navy shirt and a pair of plaid shorts fastened a good six inches below his waist.

Blake called out a greeting, and the kid responded with a wave. But instead of boarding the old Bayliner Cuddy, he approached, moving with that cocky swagger so prominent among teens and twentysomethings nowadays. He leaned against the nearest piling. "You staying in Cedar Key awhile?"

"For the time being. Why?"

"I do odd jobs. You need any work done, let me know. Name's Terrance." He took a swig of the Budweiser in his hand. Apparently he was at least twenty-one. Or someone was selling alcohol to minors.

"Will do. I heard you replaced a window for Allison yesterday."

"Yeah." He wiped his mouth on the sleeve of his shirt. "Her house got broken into. I hope they catch the guy."

Terrance turned to go, but Blake stopped him. "Speaking of Allison, did you see her leave this morning?"

"Yeah."

"Did she happen to say what time she was coming back?"

"Four."

A little early for Brinks's walk, but Brinks wouldn't mind.

Terrance lifted his beer in farewell then headed to his boat. With a cabin just big enough for a berth and toilet, the Bayliner Cuddy was built for the occasional overnight, not living aboard. But Terrance didn't seem to mind. He was independent and supporting himself. That was probably all that mattered.

Blake closed the paper and capped the Sharpie. He could spend only so many hours fishing, reading and exploring. So that was why he had circled two job postings in the classified section. A third he had looked at briefly, then decided to pass. Cedar Key Auto was looking for a mechanic. He was okay, but not good. Actually, when it came to gainful employment, he was okay at a lot of things— jack-of-all-trades, master of none. Except police work. That he was good at.

Monday he would make the two phone calls. One was The Market at Cedar Key, twenty hours a week cleaning and stocking. The other was grounds work for a landscaping outfit, also part-time. He wouldn't apply for anything that required extensive training. It wouldn't be fair to his potential employer.

As expected, Allison's boat came into view at twenty till four. By four o'clock, she had docked and was telling her charter customers goodbye. Blake stood to take the newspaper and empty glass below and don some tennis shoes. By the time he had traded Brinks's restraint for a real leash and stepped onto the dock, Allison had finished hosing down her boat.

"So how was the charter?"

"Perfect. This is my favorite time of year."

"Mine, too." His gaze swept the length of the hull and came to rest on some simple turquoise script. "*Tranquility*. Very fitting name. She's beautiful."

She looked up from her chores and flashed him a smile. "Thanks."

He watched her while she finished her end-of-the-day routine. "I'm going to be heading out to take Brinks for a walk, but I can take a different route. I don't want you to think I'm stalking you."

"That's all right. The company's kind of nice." She stepped off the boat and grinned up at him. "I'll let you know when I get tired of you."

He started down the dock next to her. "Do you have any charters tomorrow?"

"No. I try to take Sundays off. At least Sunday mornings."

"It's nice to sleep in every so often."

A gust of wind swept through and whipped her hair into her face. Several strands had come loose from the braid during her time on the water. She reached up to tuck them behind her ear.

"Actually, that's not it. I'm an early riser. Can't sleep past sunup regardless. But Sunday morning I'm usually in church, singing in the worship ensemble."

"You sail *and* you sing. Any other talents I don't know about?"

"No, that's pretty much it. My parents tried piano lessons, too, but I didn't take to them like the voice lessons."

He nodded. Somehow the singing didn't surprise him. Her voice held an almost mesmerizing quality, a smooth, low timbre that slid over him like fine silk.

"If you'd like to go, I'll be happy to pick you up."

Church? He hadn't been since age sixteen, when he decided he didn't need some stuffy old man in a robe telling him how to live his life. "I'll have to pass. I've got some things to do." He wasn't sure what, but he'd think of something.

When they reached her house, he walked with her to the door, where she stopped to give Brinks some brisk scratches on the neck and throat. Her eyes sparkled, the uneasiness he had seen yesterday gone. Finally, she straightened to give him a parting smile.

"I'll see you around."

As soon as she had unlocked and opened the door, he turned to head back to the street. But her startled gasp stopped him midstride. He spun toward her, and his stomach went into a free fall. Her face was three shades lighter than it had been moments ago, and her eyes were wide with fear.

He took two quick steps forward. "What is it?"

"Someone's been in the house."

"Are you sure?" He stepped past her into the foyer and immediately answered his own question. The top had been removed from the first stair post and was lying on the foyer floor. To the right, an open double doorway framed scattered brocade pillows. A roll of what looked like house plans had been slung against a sofa leg. Dog-eared pages curled into haphazard rolls on the polished oak floor, partially hidden by one of the sofa seat cushions.

He turned toward Allison, a sense of protectiveness surging up inside him. He couldn't help it. It was his police training. Once a cop, always a cop. Being unable to do the job didn't take away those instincts.

Allison stood in the doorway, phone in hand, calling nine-one-one. He stepped back outside, and within minutes, a Cedar Key police cruiser stopped at the curb, siren silenced. The lights remained flashing. It was Hunter, the same cop who had cuffed him early yesterday morning. The officer's eyes shifted from him to Allison and then back to him. The question in his gaze was probably about more than just the call.

Hunter stepped onto the porch and addressed Allison. "Another break-in?"

"Seems that way. Maybe it's time I install an alarm."

Blake looked at her sharply. "You don't have one? I thought you said you did." In fact, he *knew* that was what she had said.

Early yesterday morning, when Hunter had him pinned against the cruiser.

A grin climbed up her cheeks. "I didn't say I *had* an alarm. I just said I wouldn't forget to set it."

He matched her smile with one of his own. "You just wanted me to *think* you had one."

"I figured it wouldn't hurt. Just in case." She motioned Hunter inside. "I don't know how bad it is. I didn't go past the front doorway."

Blake started to follow, then hesitated. It wasn't his case. He wasn't even a cop anymore. He was a civilian getting ready to walk into a woman's house uninvited. He cast a glance at Allison. "Is it all right if I go in?"

"Sure. Another set of trained eyes can't hurt."

Hunter stopped in the doorway of the living room. "Since all the cushions are off the furniture, I'm guessing he was looking for something." He made a slow circle through the room, then pointed at the floor. "Are those house plans?"

"Yeah." Allison led him back into the foyer.

"The night after the first break-in, I noticed that this finial was crooked. Then I discovered the post is hollow. The house plans were inside." She started to rest her hand on top of the newel post, then drew back. She wouldn't touch anything until after they finished investigating.

Hunter nodded. "They sometimes did that with these old Victorians, hid the house plans in a secret compartment in the newel post."

Blake raised his brows. That was an interesting tidbit.

Allison was apparently as intrigued as he was. "You've heard of this?"

Hunter flashed her a sheepish smile. "My little sister went through a stage where she was nuts over any and all things Victorian. She collected trinkets, played dress-up in period clothes and read everything she could get her hands on. And I learned all kinds of worthless information that I'll probably never use, because she never shut up about it."

She returned his smile. "Well, it didn't turn out to be totally worthless, because you just taught me something. Now when I go into a Victorian house, I'll always wonder what might be hidden in the newel post." She chewed her lower lip, suddenly serious. "If the intruder was hoping for treasure, he probably wasn't too happy to find nothing but a roll of old house plans."

Which means he might be back. She didn't finish the sentence aloud, but she was thinking it. It was all there in her eyes. The fear and uncertainty.

Hunter stroked his chin with a thumb and forefinger, deep in thought. "Seems if he was just hoping for something in the newel post, he wouldn't have searched any further. It's as if he knew exactly what he was looking for."

He moved across the foyer toward the den. When he pushed open one of the double doors, Allison drew in a sharp breath. Blake looked over Hunter's shoulder and understood. It looked as if every file had been removed from the file cabinet, the contents emptied.

"Whoa." Hunter turned to face her. "I'd say he was pretty determined to find something."

Allison didn't respond. Blake studied her.

Maybe she was just dazed. But something told him she knew more than she was telling them.

Hunter continued his walk through the house, getting an overview before the real investigation started. When he swung open one of two mahogany doors next to the kitchen, a low whistle escaped his mouth. Blake stepped into the room, and the dusty scent of old books wrapped around him, mixed with the smell of varnish.

It was a library. Floor-to-ceiling shelves lined three walls. But they were all empty. Teetering piles of books lay on the two stuffed chairs and all over the floor. There were dozens of them, maybe hundreds.

"This is a pretty impressive library you have here."

Allison nodded. "It is. At least it *was*. The fiction was all arranged by author last name, the nonfiction categorized and labeled according to the Dewey Decimal System. But I can't take the credit. This was my grandparents' collection. Even though there have been a couple of owners in between, apparently no one has been able to part with the books."

Hunter stepped up next to him. "Are we ready to tackle this mess?"

Excitement swept through him. This was what he was made for—police work.

"Deputize me, and I'm all yours."

THREE

Allison watched the two officers work their way through her house. Hunter looked sharp and professional in his crisp navy pants and light blue polo shirt, embroidered with Cedar Key Police Department. He moved with confidence, dusting doorjambs and other surfaces, lifting prints and making note of each location.

In khaki cargo shorts and a sailboat print shirt, Blake wasn't dressed for the part, but everything else about him said cop. His dark eyes were alert as he scanned each room, and he exuded a sense of seriousness and concentrated focus. But there was something else, too—excitement and anticipation. Police work had been his life. Now she understood the fulfillment he had gained from his work. And the trauma of having it ripped from him.

A pang of tenderness shot through her. Total upheaval—she had been there.

As the two men moved toward the dining room, Blake's limp appeared more pronounced than usual. He was apparently too focused on the investigation to think about trying to hide it. He circled the room, his gaze settling briefly on each item out of place. A pinkish-tan scar extended a couple of inches below the hem of his shorts, visible proof of the injury that had ended his career. It was the *only* visible proof. His sun-kissed, muscular arms were…perfect. He obviously hadn't spent his recuperating months sitting idle.

Without warning, those observant dark eyes met hers, and heat crept up her cheeks. He responded with a knowing smile, which only made it worse. Her gaze shifted to where Hunter stood dusting the open door of her china cabinet. They still had the library to do. And then the whole second floor.

"Check this out."

Blake's words cut across her thoughts. They were probably directed at Hunter, but she moved closer to see what he had found. When he spoke again, his question was for her.

"Did you remove the screen from this window?"

She stepped up next to him. The window was on the side of the house, blocked from the view of the street by one of her moss-draped live oaks. Now that Blake had pointed it out, she saw it, too—the screen was gone.

"No, I didn't." She put her face close to the glass. Lying on the ground next to the house was the missing screen. "In fact, I just mowed two days ago. I may not have noticed it missing from the window, but I know for a fact it wasn't lying on the ground."

Hunter joined them. He hadn't made it to that side of the room yet. "Do you think this is where he gained access?"

With latex-covered hands, Blake gripped the edges of the handle and slid the window upward in its track. "I'd say that's a definite."

"But how…" She let the words trail off. It had been locked. She had checked.

In answer, Blake lowered the window and turned the latch. It barely made contact. "A little jimmying, and this would rattle right out of here. We need to look at installing some new locks."

She nodded and swallowed hard, a sudden sense of vulnerability sweeping through her. She would get some new locks installed. ASAP.

Blake had said *we*. But she always paid her way. She would hire Terrance. Or maybe do it herself. Installing window glass was beyond her level of expertise, but she could change latches, even if she had to drill holes. Over the past two years, she had acquired several new skills. And quite a few tools. And a good dose of independence.

Boarding her boat and heading for Cedar Key alone was the scariest thing she had ever done. So was taking a good chunk of the life insurance money Tom had left and purchasing the house. But staying in Providence hadn't been an option. Neither had going back to Boston to accept help from her parents. She didn't need to hear *I told you so*.

So she summoned a strength she hadn't known she had, sold most of her belongings and headed for Florida. The strength had apparently been there all along. She had just never needed it before.

She nodded at Blake. "New locks. That's a project for tomorrow."

Hunter finished processing the area, and they stepped from the room. At least there hadn't been much stuff out in the dining room. Napkins and place mats had been removed from the buffet and lay scattered about the table. But except for some china being shifted around, the mahogany hutch was pretty much as she had left it. The rest of the house was the problem. She was going to spend the next month getting everything cleaned up, reorganized and put back where it belonged.

How had she accumulated so much in two short years? She had left Rhode Island with nothing but her boat, then bought a used car and golf cart. Now she was the proud owner of a newly restored 1880s Victorian and surrounded by stuff. She knew exactly where it had come from. And it was Darci's fault. Allison met her her first week in Cedar Key, and they became fast friends. Then Darci got her hooked on yard sales, estate sales and consignment shops. Now, two years later, the place was fully furnished, her wardrobe rebuilt and her personal belongings restocked. And then some. Bargain hunting had proven to be addictive.

"Ready to tackle the upstairs?"

The question came from Hunter.

Blake gave a mock salute. "Ready when you are. You're the boss."

Allison followed them. The guest room wouldn't be bad. There wasn't much in there. Her bedroom…that was another story. She dreaded the sight—everything dragged out of her closet, drawers emptied onto the floor. Unmentionables strewn about the room.

And Blake walking through everything.

No. That was where she was drawing the line.

As Hunter entered the room, she stepped in front of Blake and planted her palm against his muscled chest.

"Stop right there."

He looked at her with raised brows but didn't respond.

"You're *not* going into my bedroom."

"Why not?" The corner of his mouth quirked, as if he was trying to stifle a grin.

"Because I said so." She made a shooing motion with both hands. "Go investigate the guest room or something."

He didn't bother to hide his mirth now. He threw back his head and laughed, a hearty belly laugh, then gave another mock salute. "Yes, ma'am."

She watched him disappear into the bedroom at the end of the hall, then steeled herself for what she would find in hers.

It was every bit as bad as she had expected. She circled through the room, stepping around the items scattered about. The mattress had apparently been picked up and dropped back down. It was hanging over one side of the box spring by six inches. Her closet was cleared out, her dresser drawers empty except for Tom's Glock.

She moved to the dresser and opened the antique jewelry box. Nothing appeared disturbed. A small sense of relief filtered through the dread, a sliver of light in the darkness.

She turned to find Hunter watching her. "Is it all there?"

"Looks like it."

He frowned. "He left your jewelry and the Glock. This isn't the work of an ordinary burglar."

No, it wasn't. Her intruder was interested in only one thing. And she needed to tell someone.

Her gaze locked with Hunter's, and in that moment, she made her decision. Regardless of what they might find, Hunter wouldn't hold it against her. And he wouldn't tell anyone. In the two years she had known him, he had done nothing but gain her respect. He was honest, hardworking and compassionate. He was even active in church—taught a middle-school boys' Sunday School class.

Her cautious trust didn't extend to Blake. He seemed all right. More than all right. But she had thought Tom was all right, too.

"I think I know what they were looking for." She spoke the words in a whisper. "I'm giving you something, but I don't want Blake to see it. I don't want anyone to know but you and Chief Sandlin."

His gaze was filled with unspoken questions. "O-kay."

"I guess the other Cedar Key officers are okay, too." But the fewer people that knew, the better. At least until she deciphered the clues. She pulled the paper from her purse and handed it to him. She didn't need to copy the information down. She had read it so many times she had it memorized. "I found this rolled up with the house plans in the newel post."

"R45 87, G45 165, R2.55 282." His gaze met hers. "What does it mean?"

"I don't know. I think my grandparents hid something. And until I know what it is, I don't want word of this getting out."

He gave a brusque nod. "Agreed."

As he refolded the sheet and slid it into his shirt pocket, relief washed through her. Whatever was significant about that information, the intruder was determined to get his hands on it. Since he had failed again, she probably hadn't seen the last of him. As long as she held on to that paper, she wasn't safe.

When she walked the two men out twenty minutes later, Hunter left, but Blake hung back. He leaned against one of the posts supporting her porch roof. "Are you going to be okay? I'll be happy to change some window latches if you tell me where I can get them."

Her eyes met his. The concern she saw there threatened to turn her into a puddle of mush on the newly painted porch floor.

She shook off the effect and squared her shoulders. "I'll be fine. I'll have Terrance do it. Or I might get a wild hair and do it myself."

He nodded. "And the clean-up, if you don't want to face all that alone, you know where to find me."

She gave him a shaky smile. It was nice of him to offer, but having him help her put all her personal belongings away seemed too intimate.

He crossed his arms over his chest. "Two break-ins in one week seems a little excessive." The words weren't phrased as a question. But it was there all the same. He was interrogating her with his eyes.

She shrugged off his penetrating gaze. She didn't owe him any explanations. "I guess there isn't anywhere exempt from crime, even Cedar Key."

"That's true. But this isn't your run-of-the-mill burglar. Any idea what he's looking for?"

It was the same question Hunter had asked. But something in Blake's tone raised her hackles. "I don't know what you're insinuating, but I'm not into anything illegal."

He didn't respond, but continued to study her. She knew that look. She had seen it often enough—narrowed gaze, head angled slightly away, mouth set in a barely perceptible frown. Suspicion. Disapproval.

A dark cloud settled over her. She had escaped all that when she boarded her sailboat and fled Providence—the suspicious glances, the relentless questioning by police. It didn't matter that she was innocent, that she had gone about her pampered life, blissfully ignorant of her husband's activities. She was guilty by association.

Would it be the same in Cedar Key? If the clues led to something illegal, some kind of contraband or dirty family secret, would she once again find herself an outcast, shunned by society?

Maybe her intruder knew that. Maybe he planned to blackmail her with the information. Or worse yet, pin something incriminating on her.

With all she had been through, nothing was out of the realm of possibility.

Blake stared at the fiberglass ceiling two and a half feet above where he lay. Thunder rumbled in the distance, a deep-toned backdrop to the lapping of water against the hull. A muted flickering filled the eastern sky.

But it wasn't the approaching storm keeping him awake. It was thoughts of Allison. He was having a hard time figuring her out. She had a sweet air of innocence about her, a wholesome, girl-next-door quality.

But she was holding back. She knew what the intruder was after. And for some reason, she didn't want to tell anyone. Although

Hunter didn't press, *he* did. And she instantly bristled. He wished he had gone about it differently. Because now there seemed to be an invisible wall between them, the tentative camaraderie they had built over the past two days strained.

What had she gotten involved in, and why wouldn't she talk to him? Had she taken something, and someone was determined to get it back? No, whatever Allison was, she wasn't a thief.

Maybe she was holding on to something with blackmail in mind. But that didn't sound like Allison, either. There was nothing cunning or deceitful about her. Whatever trouble she had found, she probably hadn't been looking for it. And now she was in over her head.

And she was scared. No matter how she tried to hide it, fear glistened in those clear blue eyes, along with an underlying vulnerability that just about made him come undone.

He heaved a sigh and turned on his left side to massage his right leg and knee. The berth was fairly comfortable. But bad weather made everything ache. That was something he had learned to live with. He refused to feel sorry for himself. The dull ache brought on by changes in barometric pressure was nothing compared to the agony he'd endured during the weeks following his injury—the multiple surgeries, the powerful antibiotic injections when infection set in and he almost lost his leg, and the weeks of intensive physical therapy once he was on the mend.

He rolled onto his back, once again stretching out. Helping the Cedar Key cop with his investigation had been good. Actually, it had been downright exhilarating. He snickered, breaking the relative silence of the cabin. No, walking into a drug king's lair and posing as a big-time dealer had been exhilarating. Working a simple B&E was not. Thinking it was meant that he'd been away from police work too long.

Maybe he should consider going back. He had progressed far beyond his doctor's best prognosis. Of course, he'd also pushed himself harder than what any sane human being would. But the result had been worth it. He'd gotten most of his strength back and was left with just a limp. And a lot of scarring. And a leg that didn't quite work the way it was supposed to.

But there were options other than desk work. Maybe investigations. Something a little less intense than narcotics. But whatever he did, he would have to be willing to carry a gun.

And use it.

He squeezed his eyes shut against the memories trying to barrel forward. Internal Affairs had cleared him. Said it wasn't his fault.

Unfortunately, he hadn't been able to clear himself.

He sat up and scooted to the end of the berth to rest his feet on the floor and met a sleek, furry body. Within seconds, Brinks was wide-awake and standing. Great. Now he would think it was time for a walk. But maybe that wasn't such a bad idea. It might help him clear his head.

He retrieved Brinks's leash from the counter in the small galley area and lifted his gaze to the wide, squat window. It offered a good view of the eastern sky, where the light show continued. Heavy cloud cover obscured the jagged streaks, which displayed in a rapid series of flashes that spanned the horizon. The storm was a long way off. It might miss Cedar Key altogether.

He slipped a T-shirt over his head and clipped the dog's leash to his collar. After snagging his tennis shoes from the floor, he headed up the companionway stairs, Brinks in the lead. Almost immediately, he was hit with a cool, salt-scented breeze. Boats rocked gently at their moorings, the rigging on the two sailboats making a soft clanging. Masts rose skyward, one a good ten feet taller than the other one. That would be *Tranquility*, Allison's boat.

He slipped a bare foot into one shoe, then let his gaze slide upward again, toward where he knew *Tranquility* rested. The boat itself was hidden from view by the MasterCraft in the next slip, but the mast stood out against the charcoal-gray sky. It swayed back and forth, moving with the gently rolling sea.

Suddenly he tensed, his back ramrod straight. From his angle, looking abeam, it was hard to tell. But the mast had just seemed to dip away from him, as if someone had climbed aboard. Was Allison out here in the middle of the night? Somehow he doubted it.

He slipped on his other shoe and yanked the laces tight, then tied Brinks off to a cleat. If there really was an intruder out there, a trained canine would be an asset. Brinks would get in his way. Or lead him on another middle-of-the-night chase.

As soon as he stepped onto the dock, he knew. Someone hadn't just boarded *Tranquility*. He had gotten off. A crouched figure moved silently up the short span of dock that ran beside the boat. When he reached the main dock, he glanced back, straightened to his full height and ran toward the marina.

Blake shot off after him. Nine chances out of ten, he was the same guy who had broken into Allison's house. Twice. If he could catch him, he could put an end to her ordeal. And maybe find out what she had to hide.

He reached the end of the dock, rounded the side of the Cedar Key Beach and Yacht Club and pounded across the asphalt. The distance between him and the intruder was expanding. The creep was losing him. He was going to get away.

Not if he had anything to say about it. He pushed himself harder, giving it all he had, forcing his leg to function the way it was supposed to. The dull ache intensified, becoming a burn, then a stabbing pain.

Too late, he realized that his center of gravity was no longer over his feet. He was toppling forward, his struggling leg unable to keep up. He thrust his hands outward and, a fraction of a second before hitting the pavement, twisted sideways to protect his knee.

He landed on his left leg and arm, skidding several inches before coming to a stop. For some time, he lay there, taking inventory. Nothing seemed to be broken. And his right leg didn't hurt any more than it normally did. He slowly sat up, and that's when the stinging throb started. His entire left side was on fire. He turned his hand over to examine it in the light of the nearby streetlamp. From palm to elbow, he was scraped and bleeding. The side of his left leg looked the same, with bits of gravel mixed with the blood.

He rose to his feet and stumbled back to the dock. There was no sense in pursuing the chase. Allison's intruder was gone. Tomorrow he would have to tell her. He had seen the creep sneaking away from her boat and given chase.

And he fell.

Embarrassment washed over him. What kind of cop was he? Couldn't even chase a criminal and stay on his feet.

What kind of man was he?

He stepped onto his boat, untied Brinks then coaxed him back down the companionway steps with the promise of jerky treats. The walk no longer had appeal. Brinks could wait till morning. He would call nine-one-one, then doctor his wounds. And leave the police work to those more capable.

A few hours ago, he was thinking of going back. It was nothing but an impossible dream. He had lost his edge. He was physically impaired. Who would want him?

He had been stupid to even consider it.

FOUR

A persistent ring split the silence of the still night. Allison pulled the spare pillow over her head, trying to block out the annoying sound, and momentarily enjoyed total silence.

Then it came again, another series of rings followed by heavy knocks. The next moment, she was totally awake, tension spiking through her. Someone was at her door.

Her eyes sought out the alarm clock sitting on her nightstand, and her tension escalated. Who would be ringing her bell at 4:00 a.m.?

She swung her feet over the edge of the bed and reached for the robe she had left hanging on the bedpost. Her heart pounded out an erratic rhythm, in spite of the continual mental reminder that burglars don't knock. *But at 4:00 a.m., friends don't, either.*

She shrugged into her robe and, for the

second time that week, reached for Tom's Glock. The cold metal felt just as lethal as before, the threat just as real.

As she tiptoed down the stairs, a third series of rings drowned out her muffled footsteps, and her heart jumped to double time. Someone stood on the other side of the door, his shadowed form barely visible through the patterned glass. A watery weakness settled in her knees, and she leaned against the varnished banister.

When she reached the foyer, she pressed herself against the wall by the door.

"Who is it?" Her voice quavered in spite of the force she tried to put behind the words.

"It's Officer Bobby."

She released a pent-up breath as all the tension flowed out of her. The Southern drawl was unmistakable. She lowered the weapon and reached for the door. But her relief dissipated before she even twisted the lock. A police officer on her steps at 4:00 a.m. couldn't be a good thing.

When she swung open the door, Bobby's eyes dipped to the weapon then back up to meet hers. "I'm sorry to bother you, but we got a call from Blake. Apparently, someone was on your boat."

Her chest clenched, and dread trickled over her. What did they do to her boat? She didn't keep valuables on there, but she did have hundreds of dollars in electronics. And they stayed locked up. Cedar Key was a low-crime place, but she didn't believe in tempting fate. The front hatch was locked from inside, and a padlock secured the main hatch.

Of course, a good set of bolt cutters would make quick work of most padlocks.

She sucked in a stabilizing breath. "I'm getting dressed and heading right over."

Bobby nodded. "I'll meet you there."

Ten minutes later, she braked to a screeching halt at the marina and jumped from her car. Bobby was already there, standing on the dock. Blake was, too. He hurried toward her, his limp pronounced. He was in pain and trying hard to hide it.

As he drew closer, it was in his face, too, visible under the glow of the marina lights. Deep creases marked the space between his brows, and his jaw held a tightness she had never seen before. It didn't take a brain surgeon to figure out what had happened. He had seen the intruder and given chase. He had overexerted himself.

And he did it for her.

Whatever anger she had felt toward him dissipated in an instant, replaced by tenderness and something else she refused to acknowledge. Blake would make a great friend. Anything beyond that was out of the question. He was in Cedar Key just long enough to find himself before going back to his real life. In the meantime, she would show him the same Old Florida hospitality that she was shown when she first arrived. Nothing more.

Besides, she had her own issues. It would be a long time before she would let down her guard enough to trust someone again. So she refused to even entertain any romantic thoughts about Blake. No matter how good-looking he was. Or how much concern filled those dark eyes. Her life was full enough without the complication of a man and his secrets.

She squared her shoulders, and her eyes met his. "So what happened?"

"I couldn't sleep, so I decided to take a walk. When I came up on deck, the guy was getting off your boat. My view of him was blocked by the boat in the next slip, but I saw your mast tilt."

She headed up the dock, and he fell in behind her, continuing his explanation.

"I think it was the same guy who broke into your house."

She cast a glance at him over her shoulder. "Why do you say that?"

"He was looking for something. I don't think he stole anything."

"You've been on my boat?"

"No, I just shined my flashlight in, and things are in a shambles."

She stepped from the dock into the cockpit, steadying herself with the boom. Blake was right. The same person who had broken into her house was probably responsible for the mess in *Tranquility*'s cabin. Brochures, charts, cushions and dishes littered the teak floor, illuminated by the beam of Blake's flashlight.

She stepped into the opening and started down the steps. The lock lay on top of the cabin, its shackle cut in two, the obvious victim of the bolt cutters she had thought about earlier.

Once inside the cabin, she flipped the switch to the battery-powered wall lamp, and soft light filled the galley. The boat tilted, and she turned to see who had just stepped on. It was Bobby.

"Does it look like they took anything?"

Her gaze circled the cabin and came to rest on the navigation station. Although the brochures she had left on the small work surface had been swept onto the floor, the instrument panel was untouched. The VHF and Garmin were exactly as she had left them. No one had even tried to remove them.

"Not that I can tell. Everything's just ransacked, like my house." She was still trying to put the place back together.

Bobby moved down the steps to stand beside her in the galley. "Someone's awfully determined to get his hands on that paper. Good thing you gave it to us. It wouldn't be too safe to have it in your possession right now."

She glanced through the open companionway to where Blake stood on the dock. Nothing in his stance indicated that he had heard Bobby's words. He stood in profile, staring out toward where Atsena Otie lay off the southern tip of Cedar Key.

"Well, I'm going to see if I can lift any prints. We didn't have much luck before. The few good ones we got don't seem to match anything in the system."

"Probably because they're mine."

She followed him off the boat, then waited on the dock with Blake while Bobby continued to his cruiser. In a few minutes he would be back with his brush and sticky black powder. By now, she should be a pro at removing it from all household surfaces.

Last night, she had worked until midnight and gotten her bedroom put back together. She had planned to reward herself by sleeping till six thirty, then enjoying a leisurely breakfast before her nine o'clock charter. So much for plans. By the time she got everything cleaned up and ready for the day, she'd be lucky to grab a Clif bar.

A weary sigh escaped, and she turned to see Blake watching her, his eyes filled with tenderness.

"Your house, and now your boat. Are you okay?"

She lifted her shoulders in a prolonged shrug. "Yeah, I'm all right. It doesn't look like he took anything, and nothing's damaged. So it could be worse."

"You must be a glass-half-full kind of lady."

"Not always. Sometimes I let life kick me around a little before I remember that it doesn't do any good to feel sorry for myself."

Bobby approached with his kit, then continued on to the boat. Instead of following, she closed her eyes, drew in a salt-scented breath and released it slowly, letting the tranquility of the night wrap around her. The last of her tension drained away with the soothing sounds of the marina—the clanging of rigging, the lapping of water and the muffled thump of boats against the rubber-lined docks. Such was the seaside—peaceful, but never silent.

She opened her eyes and smiled up at Blake. "Thank you for what you did."

He cocked a brow. "I didn't do anything."

"Yeah, you did. You tried to catch the guy."

"A lot of good it did me." His tone was thick with sarcasm and a healthy dose of self-loathing. He started to cross his arms, then winced, dropping them back to his sides.

"You're hurt." She reached for him, resting her hand against his forearm.

His muscles tensed beneath her palm, and he twisted away. "I'm fine."

For several moments, she watched him in silence. He stood silhouetted against the flickering eastern sky, his jaw set in a firm line. Apparently, whatever expectations he set for himself didn't allow for failure.

Typical man. Tom had been the same way. Shortly before he was killed, he hinted at some serious regrets, bad choices he had made. All he wanted, he had said, was to let her know how much he loved her, to give her everything she deserved. Why couldn't he see that she wasn't interested in things?

"Hey, you tried, and that's what counts. It wasn't your job *or* your boat, so you didn't have to do anything."

He turned to face her. "I really wanted to catch this guy. I thought I'd be able to put a stop to all this. Now he's still out there."

"I appreciate that. But quit being so hard on yourself." She gave him a gentle shove. "You had a total knee replacement, what, a year ago?"

"Eighteen months."

"Okay, eighteen months. If you're expecting to be able to do everything you did before, you're being unrealistic."

She glanced over at her boat, where Bobby was still hard at work, then turned her attention back to Blake.

"Don't worry. We'll catch the creep sooner or later." She tried to infuse her tone with confidence she didn't feel. "Cedar Key isn't that big, and people watch out for each other. It's just a matter of time till someone sees something."

"You're probably right." He gave her a half smile, then tilted his head toward her boat. "Do you have a charter this morning?"

"Yeah, nine o'clock."

"Are you going to be able to get everything cleaned up in time?"

She shrugged. "I don't have a choice. Usually my customers stay up on deck. But if someone needs to use the head, or just get out of the sun, they've got to be able to walk through the cabin without picking up black powder or traversing an obstacle course."

"How about letting me help you?"

"You don't need to do that."

"I know. But when I'm up, I'm up. I don't go back to sleep. So the way I look at it, I can go back to my boat and twiddle my thumbs, waiting for the sun to come up. Or I can take Brinks for a walk through the deserted streets of Cedar Key, waiting for the sun to come up. Or I can spend the next couple of hours helping a pretty charter captain clean up her boat and not even think about how long it'll be till the sun comes up."

Allison smiled as a little of the weight began to lift. "Well, when you put it that way..."

"I'll even take you to breakfast afterward."

"*I* should take *you* to breakfast."

"Before you make any promises, you'd better wait and see if I'm worth it."

Oh, he would definitely be worth it. She had no doubt. Seeing the mess in her boat was like a kick in the gut, especially knowing what she still had to deal with at home. If Blake did nothing more than lend moral support, he'd be worth the cost of a meal at Ken's. But something told her he'd do a lot more than that. His injury hadn't taken away his ambition.

She leaned back against one of the pilings and crossed her arms. Finally, Bobby emerged from the cabin with his kit.

"Sorry to leave you with a mess."

"No problem. I think we've got it under control."

When she smiled over at Blake, the warmth in his eyes created a flutter in her stomach.

Yeah, they had it under control. Within the hour, everything would be back in its place and all surfaces sparkling clean. Then she would enjoy that anticipated leisurely breakfast. In the company of Blake.

It was shaping up to be not such a bad morning after all.

Blake watched Bobby walk to his patrol car, then followed Allison onto her boat. Even with stuff strewn everywhere, it was obvious *Tranquility* was well maintained. With a good-size galley and dining area and berths fore and aft, she would make a comfortable live-aboard.

Allison bent to pick up some towels the intruder had tossed onto the floor. "I'm not sure where to begin."

"How about if we start with cleaning the galley countertop so we've got a clean surface to work with."

"That sounds like a plan." She pulled some paper towels from the roll mounted in the galley. "So, are there any inside secrets to cleaning this up?"

"I don't know how *inside* it is, but once the

loose powder is wiped up, warm, soapy water works pretty well. Not that I know firsthand."

"No, I'm sure your experience is with making the mess instead of cleaning it up."

"Not me. I was undercover narcotics. Drug buys and sting operations. No playing with crime scene kits."

She grinned up at him. "Okay. You're off the hook."

While she wiped down the countertop with dry paper towels, he ran water into the sink and added a squirt of dish detergent. Soon the mottled gray-and-white surface shined. Over the next forty minutes, he tackled the teak cabinets and other areas, and she set out returning everything to its proper place.

Finally, she stepped from the front berth into the dining area and closed the door. "Well, that's the last of it. I appreciate your help. I was feeling so overwhelmed, it would have taken me three times as long to do it by myself."

"No problem. I enjoyed it." The past hour had left him with an odd sense of contentment that he hadn't experienced in a long time. He reached up to rest his hands in the companionway opening.

Her eyes widened, and he jerked his arm down. But it was too late. She had already seen his bloodied elbow and forearm.

"You *did* get hurt."

"Just a little scrape. No big deal."

His minimizing his injuries obviously hadn't allayed her worries. Her eyes were still wide, and furrows marked the space between her brows.

"You fell. What about your knee?"

"My knee's all right. As soon as I realized I was going down, I made sure I landed on my left side."

She reached past him to remove a first-aid kit from a cabinet.

He eyed her with suspicion. "What are you doing?"

"I'm going to take care of that." She tilted her head toward his arm. "It's going to hurt like the dickens tomorrow."

What was she talking about? It already hurt like the dickens. Besides the sting of scraped skin, his elbow felt bruised to the bone. He was lucky it wasn't broken.

"You're making a big deal out of nothing. I fell, got a little boo-boo. No big deal." He averted his gaze, embarrassment washing over him anew at having to say it out loud.

She took his hand and squeezed. "Hey, it's nothing to be ashamed of."

"What do you mean?" Even as the question spilled from his mouth, he knew exactly what she meant. She could already read him like a book. It was kind of scary.

"All you guys have these preconceived notions of what makes a real man. Then when something happens and you can't live up to those impossible standards, it totally messes with your psyche." She placed the first-aid kit on the counter, opened it and began laying out scissors, gauze and antibiotic ointment, continuing to speak as she worked.

"You were injured in the line of duty. That makes you a hero in my book. That's nothing to be ashamed of."

Yeah, right. She'd change her tune in a hurry if she knew the whole story. He was no hero. Heroes brought down the bad guys without killing innocent children.

She carefully lifted his left hand and placed it against his chest, exposing the underside. "Now, let me clean this and get some ointment on it. It's the least I can do after you went all Rambo on me and tried to tackle a possible killer."

"This isn't necessary." He mumbled the words, and even he had to admit that his objections were losing their fire. He would let her do her nurturing. At least he had had the presence of mind to change into pants before she arrived, or she'd be doctoring his leg, too.

She soaked a hand towel and began cleaning his wounds. She was doing a much better job than he had. Although he had tried to pick all the small pieces of gravel out of his arm, seeing the underside of one's elbow wasn't exactly easy.

"So what happened the night you were injured? You said a drug buy went bad?" She asked the question without looking up from her work. She had finished cleaning his wounds and was applying liberal amounts of antibiotic ointment to the underside of his arm. The salve was soothing. Or maybe that was her touch.

"Yeah."

"What happened?"

He drew in a deep breath. "We were all in position, getting ready to bust a big dealer. I showed up to make the buy, not realizing my cover had been blown. The perp came out with a semiautomatic. We returned fire and took him down."

And a twelve-year-old kid had been in the wrong place at the wrong time and had paid for it with his life.

The familiar gut-wrenching guilt pressed down on him, threatening to smother him. No, he couldn't think about it now, not with Allison there. He didn't need to look up to know that she was studying him. And she would know there was more to the story.

But he couldn't talk about it. With anyone.

Besides, she had her own secrets. With a little luck, he would get to the bottom of one of them by daybreak.

Allison put the unused gauze into its pack and placed each of the items back into the first-aid kit.

"Well, I think that'll do it. My professional diagnosis is that you're going to live."

He held up a gauze-wrapped arm. "I look like a burn victim."

"What's wrong? Are you afraid it's going to mess with your macho image?"

"No problem there. The limp already has."

"I don't know about that. I'd say the limp goes quite well with the whole wounded hero persona."

"If you say so." He leaned back against the galley cabinets. "What's on the paper?"

A flash of panic shot through her eyes. "What paper?"

"The paper Bobby mentioned. Yes, I over-heard."

"What, you've got bionic hearing, too?" There was an unmistakable touch of defensiveness in her tone.

"It probably *is* better than average. So tell me about the paper. Where did it come from?"

Several seconds passed in silence. Finally, she sighed. "The newel post."

He waited for her to continue, but she didn't. She was going to make him pry it out of her. Fine.

"What newel post?"

"In my house."

"Okay. So this paper was hidden in the newel post. What did it have on it?"

"Numbers and letters. Mostly numbers."

"Any idea what they mean?"

"Not a clue."

"Did you keep a copy or write down these letters and numbers?"

"No."

For the next several moments, she didn't meet his eyes. He was pretty sure she was telling the truth. But he was equally sure there was something she was keeping from him.

"Not to scare you or anything, but what do you think this guy is going to do when he exhausts places to search? What do you think his next step will be?"

She slowly lifted her gaze and met his. Her eyes were filled with fear.

"I have no idea. I try not to think about it. Because if I did, I'd never sleep again."

FIVE

Allison's eyes shot open. The dead-of-night silence was thick—no creaks, no rattles, not even the persistent whine of the wind through the trees. But she couldn't shake the uneasiness that had fallen over her, a sense of imminent danger.

She lay sprawled on her back, unable to move. The room was shrouded in darkness, the moon and stars apparently hidden by clouds. Even the glow of the back porch light was missing. Maybe the bulb had burned out.

Or someone had unscrewed it.

She rolled her head a few degrees to the right and strained to make out her surroundings. The furnishings were little more than shadows, slightly darker than the rest of the space. On the far wall was her long dresser with the ornate mirror, next to that, her closed...

No, the door wasn't closed. It was open— just enough for someone to slip through.

She bolted upright, her startled gasp piercing the still night. There was an instantaneous flash of movement, and a gloved hand clamped over her mouth, forcing her backward onto the pillow.

Panic spiraled through her, and her heart threatened to explode through her chest. She gripped his wrist and pulled. But she was no match for his strength. Kicking and twisting only tangled her legs in the sheets. When she tried to sink her teeth into his palm, the leather glove took the brunt of it.

Then a cold steel blade pressed against her throat. The fight drained out of her. A hollow coldness settled in her core, and her mouth filled with the metallic taste of fear.

She lay still, afraid to breathe. A bead of moisture trailed toward the back of her neck. Blood. He had cut her. She resisted the urge to reach for her throat, waiting for him to make the first move. A ski mask covered his face, leaving his eyes hidden in shadow.

He bent over her, still holding the knife

against her throat. "I won't hurt you as long as you cooperate. You have something I want." His voice was a hoarse whisper. "I'm going to move my hand now. If you make a peep, I'll slice your throat from one ear to the other. Understood?"

She acknowledged his threat with a slight dip of her head. When he lifted his hand, she drew in a shaky breath.

He nodded his approval. "Now, tell me what you did with the paper."

"I don't have it."

The pressure of the blade against her throat increased. "I don't believe you. It was in the post. When I came back, it was gone."

She closed her eyes, willing herself to stay calm. One false move, and she would be dead. "I know. I took it out, but I gave it to the police."

He continued in his raspy whisper. "I don't believe you. If you value your life, you'd better give it up."

"I'm telling the truth. You've torn everything apart. If I had it, don't you think you would have found it?"

A long span passed in silence. She had obviously thrown a monkey wrench into his plans. Finally, he took the knife from her throat and turned on the lamp by her bed. What was he doing?

The next moment, she knew. He grabbed her purse from the nightstand and thrust it at her. "Empty it."

She sat up and began removing items. The front pouch held her keys and wallet. The back served as a collect-all for everything she accumulated while out. The center zippered portion held everything else. Once the contents had been removed, she tipped her purse upside down and shook it.

"Unfold the papers."

After she showed him three grocery lists, a crayon drawing from Darci's son and an advertisement for kayak rentals left under her wiper blade last week, he seemed satisfied.

"We can search my car, too." Anything to get him out of her house.

"I already did."

Her heart sank. Her house, her boat and now her car. She had left it sitting beside the house. Locked. He hadn't broken the glass, or she would have heard it.

She looked up at him, waiting for him to continue. Nothing was identifiable. Black leather gloves disappeared into the long sleeves of his shirt. Only his eyes were visible. A nondescript shade of brown. And his build. Stocky. Maybe medium height. It was hard to tell sitting in bed.

"Get up." The command came in the same gravelly whisper as his other words.

Her chest clenched. Was he planning to take her with him?

"What?"

"I said get up."

She scurried from the bed and reached for her robe.

"Leave it."

"Shoes?"

In response, he grabbed a fistful of her hair and propelled her toward the door.

God, help me. He *was* taking her with him. He was going to hold her for ransom until someone turned over the paper.

When they reached the bottom of the stairs,

he directed her toward the kitchen. At the back door, he hesitated.

"Now kneel."

She dropped to her knees on the porcelain tile floor, her mind racing. Was he planning to kill her? She didn't give him what he wanted, so he was going to execute her?

Instead of slitting her throat, he shoved her forward until the side of her face rested against the cold hard surface, her knees and arms trapped beneath her chest.

"Now, count slowly to a hundred. Don't move until you're finished." He unlocked and swung open the back door. A second later, it closed with the softest thud.

Except for the pounding of her heart, the next several minutes passed in silence. Finally, she pulled herself to her feet, clutching the cabinet for support. She hadn't counted. If she had, she would have reached a hundred long before she found the courage to stand.

She relocked the back door and headed upstairs. She needed to call the police. And she needed to secure her house. She had changed out the original locks. There had only been seven. The others had been replaced sometime before she moved in. There was no way they could be jimmied. The latch turned a full one hundred eighty degrees, burying itself in the opposing track. And both doors had dead bolts.

But he had still gotten in.

From now on, she was sleeping with the Glock under her spare bed pillow.

A distant siren pierced the night, bringing Blake instantly awake. In the city, they were so commonplace he tuned them out.

Not in Cedar Key. In his experience, a siren in Cedar Key usually involved Allison.

He sprang from the berth, and his body immediately screamed in protest. He was still sore from his tumble two nights ago.

Ignoring the pain, he shrugged into a T-shirt and jeans and slipped on his tennis shoes. When he stepped off the dock, he headed straight to the bicycle he had left parked by a tree.

Yesterday morning while Allison was in church, he'd stumbled upon a garage sale. So late in the weekend, most of what was left was junk, the bike included. But it would come in handy. Although everything was within walking distance, taking the bike would be faster. And at five bucks, he couldn't beat the cost. He hadn't bothered with a chain and lock. Given the condition it was in, he would have to pay someone to steal it.

He threw his bad leg over the bar and settled onto the seat. Two minutes later, he braked to a stop in front of Allison's house. A patrol car sat at the edge of the street, its lights strobing red and blue. Her front door was unlocked. He pushed it open and called her name.

"Back here."

Not knowing where *here* was, he headed toward the back of the house, glancing into the rooms he passed. She had made good progress putting the place back together. The living room looked ready to entertain guests. The couch cushions were where they belonged, and nothing covered the floor except a green-and-dark-pink area rug. The dining room was spotless, as was the kitchen. That was where he found Allison and Hunter.

An unexpected rush of relief swept through him on seeing her. His gaze moved to Hunter. "Did someone try to break in again?"

"He didn't just *try*. He succeeded. I'm still trying to figure out how."

Hunter moved past him to head down the hall, and Allison turned to face him fully. A jolt traveled all the way to his toes. Her hair flowed over her shoulders in wild cascades, and her skin didn't hold much more color than the ivory robe fluttering about her ankles. Haunted blue eyes locked on to his, a silent cry for help.

A fierce sense of protectiveness surged through him, and he took three brisk steps toward her before he caught himself. The crushing hug he longed to give her would be more for his sake than hers. He settled instead for a comforting hand on her shoulder.

"Are you all right? Did he hurt you?"

"I woke up, and he was in my room." Her voice was paper thin, with an uncharacteristic waver. Fear still lingered in her eyes.

A cold lump slid down his throat and settled in his gut. His gaze flicked over her. There were no obvious injuries except...an inch-long horizontal red line marked one side of her throat. Blood had beaded along its length.

His chest tightened. "What happened to your neck?"

"He put a knife to my throat and demanded to know what I had done with the paper."

He clenched his fists, fury pumping through him. No wonder she was so pale. "What did you tell him?"

"I told him I gave it to the police. He didn't believe me at first."

"Does he now?"

"I think so. He's searched everything I own. Tonight he made me empty my purse, and he went through my car."

"Was it locked?"

She nodded. "Hunter said he used one of those slim jim tools. It messed up the rubber strip along the bottom of the window." She drew in a shaky breath. "Anyway, when I told him I didn't have the paper, he seemed to not know what to do. He made me come downstairs and kneel on the floor. I thought he was going to kill me."

Her voice cracked, and she blinked several times, her eyes suddenly moist. The terror of this night would stay with her a long time. He squeezed her shoulder, longing to somehow take it from her.

"What happened then?"

"He left."

"You told him you didn't have it, and he just left?" That didn't sound like someone who was experienced in persuading people to talk.

"He said to stay on the floor until I had counted to a hundred. When I got up, he was gone. But I don't think he was giving up. He was just stepping back to regroup."

His insides melded into a solid tangle of worry. "You're not safe here. Is there anywhere you can go until we catch this guy?"

"We?"

She had a point. Her protection was Cedar Key's responsibility. But he had made it his, too.

She shook her head. "Anywhere I go, he's going to find me. Cedar Key's not that big."

"Then you need twenty-four-hour police surveillance."

"With three full-time and three part-time officers, I don't think that's going to happen. But I'm sure they won't mind driving by and keeping an eye on my place. Hunter and Bobby are already doing that. So is Chief Sandlin." Judging from the lack of confidence in her tone, the occasional drive-by wasn't giving her the security she longed for.

"What about in between patrols?"

"I'll be sleeping with the Glock."

"Do you know how to use it?"

"No, but I was hoping you'd teach me."

Her words triggered that familiar tightening in the chest that hit him every time he thought about handling a weapon. "Shooting lessons are a great idea. But there are people who can teach you who are more qualified than I am."

She stared at him, jaw slack in disbelief. "More qualified than a cop?"

Before he could respond, Hunter's voice came from the top of the stairs. "Allison? You'd better come and look at this."

Blake followed Allison into the foyer and up the stairs. Maybe Hunter had figured out how the intruder had gained access. Even though Allison had changed out the old window latches, the creep had gotten in anyway. Whether she wanted him to or not, he wasn't leaving until he had checked every lock in the place. And changed any he wasn't happy with.

Hunter led them into the guest room. On the far wall, a French door and window looked out onto a balcony. The window was open.

Allison gasped. "But how..." She let the thought trail off. "The window was locked. I'm sure of it."

Hunter crossed the room and bent to retrieve some objects from the floor. "You're right. In fact, the lock is still latched. It's just not attached to the window."

He showed them what he held. A completely functional lock and four small screws lay in one latex-covered palm. "The screws are obviously too short to go through the latch and into the wood. You'll probably find some outlet covers with missing screws."

Blake frowned. "When he was inside ransacking the house, do you think he swapped out screws so it would look like it was secure, but wasn't?"

Hunter nodded. "That's exactly what I think. Then all he had to do was shimmy up one of the balcony posts, remove the screen and lift the window. He was in with hardly a sound."

Allison shook her head, shock still etched into her features. "I looked at all the latches in the house. If they were the new style, I knew they were secure and didn't even check."

"Well," Hunter began, "you were half right. These *are* good, solid locks. Unfortunately, if they're not securely attached to the window, they're worthless."

Blake walked through the upstairs, checking outlets. As expected, four covers were missing screws, two in the guest room, one in the bathroom and one in Allison's bedroom. The longer screws had disappeared.

Hunter turned to Allison. "It's a long shot, but since he may have handled this previously, I'm going to see if I can lift any prints from the latch itself. Otherwise, I'll spare you the pleasure of the messy black powder."

"I appreciate that."

"Then we need to get that reattached. I'd like to check the other locks, too, just to make sure they're secure."

"I wasn't going to leave without seeing to that myself." Blake cast a teasing glance at Allison. "Unless she throws me out."

Allison held up both hands in surrender. "Check to your heart's content. It'll only make me feel better." She crossed her arms in front of her and looked up at Hunter. "Any luck deciphering what I gave you?"

One brow lifted in question.

"Yeah, he knows. Bobby mentioned it, and he overheard."

Hunter cast him a conspiratorial glance. "I'm a pretty good judge of character. I think you can trust him."

Blake smiled. It was good having Hunter in his corner. His word seemed to carry a lot of weight with Allison. Since Hunter thought he was okay, Allison thought he was okay. And for some reason, that mattered.

Hunter heaved a sigh. "I haven't figured anything out yet. I've shown it to the other officers. Some ideas have been tossed around, but nothing we could really go with."

Allison looked up at Blake, and one side of her mouth cocked up. "How good are you at puzzles?"

"I'd say I'm as good as the next person."

"Then follow me."

She turned and padded down the stairs, her robe flowing out behind her, a pool of ivory silk. As Hunter headed out to retrieve his fingerprint kit, Allison swung open the double doors to the den. Inside was total chaos. She obviously hadn't gotten there yet.

She crossed the room to pull a sheet out of the printer, sidestepping the papers and file folders slung about. After scrawling three lines, she handed him the page. "What do you make of this?"

He skimmed the lines. "I thought you said you didn't know the numbers."

"You asked if I had made a copy of the paper or written down the numbers. I said no, which was the truth. I didn't write them down until just now."

"You're sneaky."

"No, I'm not." She flashed him a sassy grin. "You just don't ask the right questions."

"I'll be sure to make them more pointed in the future."

He lowered his gaze to the page he held. R45 87, G45 165, R2.55 282. Finally, he looked back up at Allison. "Not a clue. This is going to take some thought. Can I have this?"

Allison nodded. "Just be careful. Someone wants that awfully bad."

Yeah, bad enough to hold a knife to her throat. "I'm going to make sure the house is secure, but you really need an alarm system."

"I thought about it after the first break-in."

"Good. The sooner you get it installed, the better. And a good guard dog wouldn't hurt. But I suppose that's out of the question."

"I actually thought about that, too. A Rottie at the foot of my bed would be pretty comforting. But I don't know what I'd do with him during the day."

He frowned. He could offer to move in and sleep on her couch. But he knew the answer to that without asking. He would have to settle for the alarm. And the secure locks. And the regular patrols. And the Glock. Today he would make some calls and get her enrolled in a basic pistol class.

But there was only one surefire way to take Allison out of danger.

Make sense of those numbers.

SIX

Allison sat in the living room, legs stretched out on the brocade sofa and back resting against one padded arm. Her iPad sat in her lap, completely at odds with the nostalgic air of the turn-of-the-century furnishings.

She loved her whole house. But if she had to choose a favorite area, this would be it. The room exuded a rich warmth, with rose-tinted walls framed by walnut wainscoting beneath and heavy crown molding above. The fireplace at the far end had yet to house a fire, at least by her hands, but the elaborate walnut chimney breast had been the source of many compliments.

She stretched her arms upward, then dropped her gaze back to the modern-day technology in her lap. She had found the Levy County property appraiser's website and located her house. The sales history supported what she had been told by the real estate agent. Her grandparents bought the place in the early forties. Eventually, they had gone into assisted living, and when they died, the house had gone to her aunt.

That was when life for the Winchesters started its downward spiral. Her uncle ran off with a younger woman, and her aunt deeded the house to her cousin and took off. Actually, that was information she had *before* talking to the real estate agent. She was sixteen when her dad got the call. He and her aunt hadn't been close, but when her life fell apart, Marilyn Winchester Morris reached out to her brother.

Sandra Morris hadn't reached out to anybody. Whatever her reasons, after a year of owning the house, she washed her hands of the whole thing, and no one had seen hide nor hair of her since. Three years later, the house went for a few thousand in unpaid property taxes.

Maybe she had learned something. Maybe she had found the paper and deciphered the numbers. And hadn't wanted to be around for the fallout.

Allison frowned. She needed to locate her cousin. She would start with her dad. He might know the whereabouts of her aunt. Then her aunt could put her in touch with her cousin. One of them ought to be able to shed some light on the cryptic message in the newel post.

She returned her gaze to the tablet. After the ridiculously low price from the tax sale was one more entry. Two years ago, to Allison Winchester, also at a ridiculously low price. She had reaped the financial benefits of the prior two owners' neglect.

She drew in a deep breath and clicked off the site. She wouldn't check out the investor who owned the house between her and her cousin. He never occupied it.

Her stomach growled, reminding her of the chicken thawing in the kitchen sink and that 6:00 p.m. was approaching fast. She had just set the iPad aside when the doorbell rang. A knot of tension formed in her stomach, and her pulse rate picked up several notches. All her visitors lately had been criminals. Or police officers with bad news.

She moved to the living room window and pushed aside the sheers to peer through the miniblinds. Two figures stood on her porch, one human, one canine. She swung open the door. Blake held Brinks's leash in one hand. A plastic grocery bag hung from the other.

A teasing smile climbed up his cheeks the moment his eyes met hers. "I'm here to discuss joint custody."

"What? Joint custody of whom?"

"Him." He pointed to the Doberman at his side. "Can I come in?"

She backed away from the door to allow them to enter. What crazy idea had he come up with now?

He stepped into the foyer. "Remember when you said a Rottie at the foot of the bed would be comforting?"

"I wasn't serious."

"Sure you were." He pushed the door shut behind him and removed Brinks's leash. "The only drawback was that you didn't know what to do with him during the day."

"I don't know what I'd do with him at night, either." Whether or not she was home was irrelevant. Bathing, feeding, walking, dog hair all over the house—she wanted no part of it. Although with Brinks's short coat, he probably didn't do a whole lot of shedding.

Blake shrugged. "Brinks isn't exactly a Rottie. Actually, he's a pretty sorry excuse for a Doberman. But think how much safer you'd feel having him here."

"You're trying to give me your dog?"

"Not *give* him to you. Just *share* him with you. I get days, you get nights." He flashed her a crooked grin. "And I'm sure we can come to an amicable agreement regarding holidays."

She shook her head. He was nuts. "I don't need a dog. I'm having an alarm installed. It's already scheduled."

"When?"

She sighed. "Friday."

"That's four days from now. In the meantime, you need Brinks. Come on. Look at him. He likes you."

She glanced down at the Doberman, who

stood staring up at her. As if to confirm, his tail nub tipped side to side in a semiwag.

"He won't be happy staying with me. He's used to being with you."

Blake's features seemed to relax. He could probably tell she was weakening. "Not really. I've only had him a month. I rescued him from the pound."

She dropped to one knee to scratch his neck. Maybe it wouldn't be too bad. If Blake had days, most of the care would fall on him. She would be responsible for breakfast. And walking him in the morning.

She straightened with a sigh. "All right. But I'm warning you. If he decides to start gnawing on my antique furniture or lifting his leg on my walls, he's all yours."

A wide grin spread across his face. "Don't worry, he's totally housebroken, hasn't had any accidents. At least not lately. And he's past the chewing stage." He reached to run a hand down the dog's back. "As long as there are no cats in the vicinity, he's a really good dog. They tell me he even had papers. His owner probably got rid of him because of that funky right ear."

She started to walk toward the kitchen, knowing Blake and Brinks would follow. "I don't have anything to feed him. But I assume that's what you're holding."

"I came prepared." He plopped the plastic bag on the counter.

Her stomach rumbled again. Now it was past six. "Has he had his supper yet?"

"Not yet. I figured I'd do it here, so you know how much to give him."

He reached into the bag and removed a porcelain dish with a painted bone in the bottom. A can came out next, and when he popped its top, Brinks perked up. The instant Blake put the bowl on the floor, Brinks plowed into the gravy-covered meat chunks as if he hadn't eaten in a week.

Allison shifted her gaze from the dog to Blake. "And how about you? Have you had supper yet?"

"No. I was going to go back to the boat and scrounge something up once I left here. Or go out if I was feeling exceptionally lazy."

"Well, this isn't The Island Room, but if you'd like to stay, I'm fixing chicken and rice."

"Chicken and rice sounds good."

She turned on the faucet and squirted a dab of soap into her palm.

Blake did the same. "What can I do to help?"

"That closet over there is the pantry." She tilted her head that direction then bent to take a pan out of the cabinet. "There's a bag of rice on the second shelf. Measure me out one cup."

As he poured rice into the measuring cup she had placed on the counter, she cast a sideways glance at him. He actually looked comfortable. She wasn't used to that. Tom had avoided the kitchen as if it was a game preserve during hunting season and he was a deer.

She opened a dry bin. "You like onions?"

"I like everything except canned asparagus and liver."

"Well, you won't find either of those here. Fresh asparagus, maybe."

Within a few minutes, the chicken had reached a rolling boil and the onions were sautéing. Brinks had long finished his dinner and was lying down, watching them from across the room.

She laid the wooden spoon on the stove next to the skillet. "Thanks."

"For what?"

"For him." She shot the Doberman another glance. "I'm going to rest a lot easier knowing he's with me...even if he would lick an intruder to death. The intruder doesn't know that. It's sweet of you to loan him to me." Blake was thoughtful in a lot of ways. If she wasn't careful, she was going to find herself caring for him much more than she should.

"No problem. I'll be resting easier, too, knowing you're not alone."

Her eyes locked with his, and the warmth there made her chest tighten. Yes, it would be so easy to fall for him.

She pushed the thoughts aside and turned to add water and rice to the onions, then checked the chicken. Once she was sure dinner was progressing as planned, she leaned back against the counter.

Blake eased onto one of the stools at the island. "So who all knows about the paper?"

"Just you and the Cedar Key Police Department. And some guy with a ski mask who's determined to get his hands on it."

"Maybe you ought to let some other people in on it, you know, your friends. The more brains involved, the better chance of solving this thing."

"No." The word came out sharper than she had intended. She softened her tone. "Until I know where this is going to lead, I don't want it out there."

"Why not?"

"What if my family was involved in something illegal?" She pushed herself away from the counter and began to pace. "What if we decipher the clues and they lead to some kind of contraband? Or a body? My life here will be over."

"How? Even if your family *was* involved in something illegal, what's that got to do with you?"

Nothing. And everything. "I'm a Winchester. When it comes down to it, that's all that will matter."

"You don't think very highly of your friendships here, do you?"

She stopped pacing and returned to stir the rice. Blake didn't understand. He would never understand unless he knew her past.

And that wasn't going to happen.

Beyond the fact that she was widowed, no one in Cedar Key knew her past. And the last person she was going to tell was Blake. She couldn't bear to see his warm brown eyes fill with condemnation. Or worse yet, pity for the stupid, gullible woman who had been too naive to see what was right in front of her.

Blake was a kind man, a good cop and a great friend. And keeping secrets from him didn't feel right. But something told her she wasn't the only one with secrets.

He was keeping a few of his own.

Blake walked down Dock Street whistling a tune, a loaded plastic bag swinging from one hand. The weather was perfect. Although the sun was almost directly overhead, it wasn't uncomfortable. An early cold front somewhere up north had left Cedar Key with paradiselike daytime temperatures in the low seventies.

Yesterday, he'd applied for two jobs. This morning he received a call from The Market offering him the position there. It was a far cry from police work, but would help alleviate his boredom.

But there was another reason for his cheeriness. Allison was taking him sailing. He had presented the request as a charter customer. Although she was appreciative of his help, she shied away from anything that smacked of romance. And that was okay. Remaining on a friendship-only basis was the safest way to go.

He couldn't deny it—she had piqued his interest from the moment he met her. She was spunky enough to sail the waters around Cedar Key solo, resolute enough to tackle putting her house back together alone and resourceful enough to install new window locks and complete other projects without help.

But beneath the self-sufficient air was an underlying fragility. When he tried to pry, her guard went up, and she closed herself off. Sometime in the past, someone had hurt her. Deeply.

And that was why he refused to involve her in a casual romance. Whatever trauma she had experienced, he wouldn't add to her pain.

He continued down Second Street, headed toward Cedar Cove. His route took him past the city park. This weekend, it would be packed with people, booths offering freshly made seafood and a local live band performing in the pavilion. According to several flyers around town, it was Cedar Key's annual Seafood Festival, an event not to be missed.

As soon as he stepped onto the dock, Allison waved to him from the deck of her boat. He held up the plastic bag.

"Lunch, provided by Tony."

As promised, he had walked to Tony's Seafood Restaurant and picked up lunch to go— salads, bread and two bowls of Tony's famous clam chowder. Everyone said Tony's chowder was the best. He would soon find out.

Allison took the bag from him. "You're bringing Brinks, right?"

He turned toward his boat, where Brinks stood looking out one of the windows. The dog responded with three enthusiastic barks. He deserved to go—based on what Allison had said that morning, he had been perfectly well behaved all night.

Blake grinned. "He was just waiting for you to ask. I'll go get him."

When he returned, Allison held out a hand to help him aboard. "It should be perfect sailing weather. Clear skies and a steady twelve-knot wind." She handed him a life jacket, one of those big, orange things that he had always hated as a kid. His dad had made him wear one every time he got on the boat, even though he had been a strong swimmer since finishing kindergarten.

"Do I really have to wear this thing?"

"I won't make you wear it, but keep it in easy reach. Brinks needs a safety line, though."

He gave her a salute. "Aye, Captain."

This was the professional Allison, the capable charter captain. Once away from Cedar Key, maybe she would let down her guard and give him a glimpse of the personal Allison, relaxed and friendly, without the restraints of professionalism or the threat of danger hanging over her head.

Yesterday, he had signed her up for a basic pistol class. The problem was, it wasn't scheduled to start for another three weeks. He was actually considering taking her to a shooting range himself. There was one in Chiefland, a little more than a half hour away. But a few trips to the shooting range wouldn't prepare someone who was afraid of guns to adequately defend herself.

Allison tied a small line around Brinks's chest, securing the other end to a cleat near the stern, then pushed the ignition button on the motor. The outboard hummed to life. "I'll get us under way. Then we'll break out lunch."

After untying the lines, she maneuvered around the other boats moored there and headed toward open sea. Brinks settled onto the seat, facing forward, sniffing the salty breeze. Excitement rippled through him.

Allison smiled down at the Doberman. "It looks as if he likes sailing."

"He likes going, regardless of the mode of transportation—car, truck, powerboat, sailboat. Plane and train we haven't tried, but he'd probably like those, too."

She stepped forward to turn a winch near the companionway hatch, and the mainsail climbed the mast. When she pulled the line attached to the boom, the sail stopped flapping. The boat tipped a good ten degrees. After killing the motor, she unfurled the front sail, and they tilted another ten degrees. Brinks stiffened slightly, then shifted position and relaxed.

The angle apparently didn't bother Allison. She stood at the wheel, left leg bent to compensate, the fabric brim of her boat hat flopping in the breeze. The usual thick braid hung down her back. Her shorts were similar to what she had worn on other occasions— cool, comfortable and modest length, and, as usual, the light blue button-up shirt was knotted at the waist. Apparently that was her standard charter attire.

The mainsail began to flap, and she adjusted the wheel, creating an almost imperceptible increase in speed. "Have you ever sailed?"

"No. I grew up around power boats, and that's all I've ever had."

"What do you think so far?"

He drew in a deep breath and let his head fall back. The triangular piece of white cloth rose skyward, its point ending far above the deck. Beyond that was blue sky, dotted with clouds. The only sounds were the wind whooshing past the sails and the rush of water flowing against the hull. The appeal of sailing was obvious. Especially with a beautiful woman. Whoever said sailing was romantic wasn't lying. Of course, romance would be the last thing on Allison's mind.

He met her gaze. "Power boats get you there faster, but this is a lot more peaceful."

She slowly turned the wheel, letting the lines out on both sails, and the boat came around. According to the compass, they were now headed due north. On this tack, the heel angle was much less.

"What do you say we break out that clam chowder?" She settled herself onto the seat next to him and propped one sneaker-clad foot against the wheel.

He reached into the plastic bag and handed her two Styrofoam containers, a round one filled with hot chowder and a square one with salad. He hadn't thought he was hungry until he had walked into Tony's and smelled the tantalizing aromas. And he had been dying to dig in ever since. On taking the first spoonful, flavor exploded in his mouth. Spicy. It was delicious.

He looked up to find Allison watching him. "You like it?"

"Mmm. No wonder it's famous."

He took another bite and looked around them. Several boats dotted the water, bobbing in the waves, their occupants fishing. One boat motored toward the open Gulf, nose pointed at an upward angle, a spray of water behind. Another seemed to be heading the same direction he and Allison were. Soon it would overtake them. Sailboats were graceful and beautiful, but they weren't fast.

"How long have you had your boat?"

"Four years. We bought it up in Rhode Island."

"We?"

"Yeah, my husband and I."

His spoon stopped halfway to his mouth, and his heart sank. *Husband? Not ex?* How had he missed that? "You're married?"

"Widowed. He was killed."

"I'm sorry to hear that." Maybe that was why she was so guarded. Maybe she was still grieving. "How long ago?"

"Two and a half years."

She didn't volunteer any further information, and he didn't ask. She was a private person. That much he had gathered. But her simple *He was killed* raised a lot of questions. What happened to him, and why was she keeping it a secret? If it was an accident, she would have said so. If he was a military man killed in combat, she would have mentioned that, too.

"So how did you get your boat down here?"

"I sailed it."

"By yourself?"

"Of course."

She acted as if it was no big deal. But single-handing a sailboat from New England to Florida was an impressive accomplishment. That would be something like twelve hundred miles.

No, farther than that. "You would have had to sail around the tip of Florida."

She grinned over at him. "Yep. There's no Florida Canal."

Okay, sixteen hundred miles. "I'm impressed."

"I took my time. Mostly stayed in the Intracoastal."

"It's still impressive. You're a pretty resourceful lady."

When they had finished eating, she held the bag open while he stuffed all their trash into it. Then he tied it up and sought out the boat he had noticed earlier. It should have passed them by now.

Instead, it was still behind them, holding the same distance, not moving closer or falling off. *What powerboat maintains a steady five or six knots?* Uneasiness sifted over him. Was this person watching her every time she went out on the water?

Allison dropped her foot and stepped back up to the wheel. "You want to give it a try?"

"Sure. I have no clue what I'm doing, but if you can do it with your foot, I should be able to handle it with both hands."

"Bring us around that way. I'm going to take us out farther."

As the nose of the boat came around, she picked up the line to the front sail and pulled, bringing it more in line with the side of the boat, then did the same with the mainsail. The boat again tilted sideways.

"Tell me what you're doing."

"The closer you sail to the wind, the more tightly you sheet the sails, and the farther we heel."

Suddenly the sails began to flap violently, and the boat righted itself.

"Whoa, not that close." She put her hand over his. "Back off some. You have to stay about forty-five degrees off the wind."

A few seconds later, the sails filled and the boat heeled.

"Okay, there. Feel it?"

He wasn't sure what he was supposed to feel. She was standing so close, her hand still over his, her arm pressed against his all the way down. It was hard to focus. Was she as aware of him as he was of her? Probably not.

She dropped her hand. "You can feel it in the wheel where you need to be."

"If you say so."

But with another thirty minutes of sailing, he understood.

"So your other charter customers, do you bring them out this far?"

"Actually, no."

"I must be special."

She grinned. "You're a special case, but that isn't necessarily a good thing."

He laughed and poked her in the ribs, and she twisted away from him. Just as he had hoped, he was starting to see the real Allison. And he liked what he was seeing.

He redirected his thoughts and focused on sailing. The swells were bigger out here and farther apart. But *Tranquility* had no problem maneuvering them. She glided smoothly up one side and down the other.

He turned around to see how far they had come. The coastline was visible in the distance. Just barely. So was something else—the boat he had seen earlier. Now he had no doubt. They were being followed.

"Do you have any binoculars?"

"Yeah. Why?"

"See that boat?" He cast a glance behind them. "It's been following us all afternoon."

Her head swiveled around, and when her eyes again met his, they were wide with worry. "Are you sure? I mean, maybe he just happens to be going the same way we are."

"I'm positive. He was following us when we were headed north, paralleling the coast. Now that we're on a west-northwest heading, he's still there, matching our speed and everything. It can't be coincidence."

She trapped her lower lip between her teeth and headed below for the binoculars. When she returned, she handed them to him and took the wheel.

He lifted them to his face and turned until what he was looking for filled the circular lenses. The boat was white. Like almost every other boat out there. If there was a name on it, he couldn't see if from that angle. Probably wouldn't be able to see it from that distance, either, even with the binoculars. A single figure stood at the helm.

"What do you see?"

"White boat, looks like only one person. That's all I can see."

He lowered the binoculars.

When her eyes met his, she still had her lower lip between her teeth. "We should probably be heading back."

"My thoughts exactly." On a sailboat several miles out was a vulnerable place to be.

She turned the boat into the wind, and it slowed to an almost dead stop before coming around and again catching the wind. The boom swung across, and she sheeted the front sail on the other side. The other boat did a complete one-eighty. As expected.

Allison looked up at him, her eyes filled with respect. "You're pretty observant."

"It's my job to notice things."

And he was making it his job to catch this guy.

The moment he learned an intruder had come into her house, those protective instincts had kicked in. But when the creep came into her bedroom and put a knife to her throat, he crossed a line.

Blake was determined to bring him down.

SEVEN

Allison sat on the living room couch, legs curled under her and phone lying in her lap. She had just finished an hour-long conversation with her mom. Brinks lay relaxed, but attentive, at her feet. Contrary to Blake's expectations, he seemed to take his assignment as guard dog seriously, refusing to leave her side from the time he arrived in the evening until Blake picked him up in the morning.

She leaned forward to give him a pat and laid her phone on the coffee table. She and her mom had done the usual catching up. The ultimate social butterfly, her mom's schedule was a flurry of activity—ladies' golf on Tuesdays, bridge on Thursdays and numerous other engagements that never let up.

Allison frowned. At one time, she had

been a part of that—active, well liked and respected by the people who "matter." Then came Tom's murder, and she had gone from socialite to pariah overnight. At least when Tom's criminal activities became public, she was living far enough from her parents that their circles of friends didn't overlap. So her mom was able to maintain her place in Boston society without the whispers and sideways glances.

She stretched out her legs and, crossing them at the ankles, rested them on the coffee table next to her phone. After getting a rundown on her mom's activities, she had told her about the break-ins, even mentioning that she now had a part-time dog. Which required telling her about Blake, something she instantly regretted. When her mom was involved, every conversation eventually cycled around to *You know, honey, it's been almost three years...*

The fact that she had no interest in dating seemed to bother her mother to no end, and no matter how much she insisted there was nothing between her and Blake except friendship, the note of hope in her mother's voice was unmistakable.

Unfortunately, her mom didn't have her aunt's number, but her dad might. It was a start. If she could get a hold of her aunt, she would be able to speak with her cousin.

Brinks suddenly tensed, and a low growl rumbled in his throat.

Allison swung her feet to the floor. "What's the matter, boy?" Although she tried to keep her tone light, a distinct note of tension underlined her words. Anything that made Brinks uneasy made her uneasy.

The dog rose to his feet and stood straight and stiff, facing the front door. Suddenly he charged toward the foyer amidst a frenzy of ferocious barking. A half second later, the doorbell rang.

Allison pushed herself to her feet and moved toward the living room window. Her heart thudded in her chest, but she managed to hold the panic at bay. There was something comforting about a growling Doberman with bared teeth. Brinks was a better security system than Blake gave him credit for.

She moved the sheer curtains and miniblinds aside and glanced over at the porch. A breath she hadn't realized she had been holding spilled out in sudden relief. Blake.

She dropped the edge of the curtain and hurried into the foyer. "It's okay, Brinks."

The dog quit barking, but the low growl continued until she opened the door. Finally convinced that it was in fact okay, Brinks stepped forward and nuzzled Blake's hand.

A seed of worry sprouted in her gut. "Is my boat okay?"

"Your boat's fine. I came because I had an idea."

"At nine o'clock at night?"

"Hey, I take 'em when I can get 'em."

She backed away and motioned him inside. "So what's your idea?"

"The numbers." He pushed the door shut behind him and locked it. "I've been racking my brain trying to figure out what they might mean."

Anticipation coursed through her. "Yes?"

"We know they're not coordinates. They're too high. But I think I might have it." He was talking fast, excitement shining in his eyes. "You believe the paper was put there by your family, right?"

"Right."

"What do you have here, left by your family, with lots of numbers?"

Her eyes widened. "The library."

"Bingo. All those books, each of them numbered. And pages within the books numbered."

She pursed her lips. "What about the letters? We've got two *R*s and a *G*."

"Maybe the author's last name?"

She spun away from him and headed toward the library at a half jog. Fortunately, she had just finished getting the books organized and back onto the shelves yesterday.

She moved to the corner and started on the top shelf, running an index finger along the bindings. *Thirty, thirty-one, thirty-two.* She dropped her hand. After thirty-two, it jumped straight into the sixties. Most of the eighties were missing, too.

"There's no forty-five. Or eighty-seven, for that matter."

"Do you have a computer and internet access?"

"My laptop is on my desk in the den."

By the time he returned, she had moved to the far end of the side wall. "The Catholic Church."

"What?"

"Two hundred eighty-two in the Dewey Decimal System is apparently the Catholic Church. This one is *History of the Catholic Church*." She pulled a book off the shelf and thumbed through it. There didn't appear to be any papers tucked inside. She put it back on the shelf and pulled out another one. "There are two more: *A History of the Popes* and *Catechism of the Catholic Church*. But none of the authors have *R*s or *G*s for initials."

She checked each of them anyway. Nothing was tucked between the pages, not even a bookmark. She glanced over at Blake, who sat at the desk, staring at the computer screen.

"What are you looking up?"

"The Dewey Decimal System. Wikipedia has the entire list."

"Find anything interesting?"

"Well, I know why you struck out on the lower numbers. Eighty-seven is collections in Slavic languages. Your grandparents likely didn't speak Russian or Polish."

"No, I'm afraid we're English, with a little German mixed in. Not a lick of Russian or Polish that I know of." She put the Catholic Church book back on the shelf. "What about forty-five?"

"There is no forty-five. Forty is unassigned, and from there it goes into the fifties—magazines, journals and serials."

"Maybe the eighty-seven and forty-five are page numbers." She pulled down the first book she had looked at and skimmed page eighty-seven. It didn't hold anything that could possibly lead to buried treasure. Forty-five didn't, either.

She checked each of the other two books and put the last one back on the shelf. "I'm not coming up with anything. If there's something here, it's really obscure."

"There's still one hundred sixty-five, but at this point, I'm not holding out much hope. One sixty-five is…fallacies and sources of error."

She took two steps to her right and located the number. There was just one book. She pulled it off the shelf. "*Exegetical Fallacies.* Sounds deep." It didn't offer any more help than the others had. She sighed and plopped down on the couch. "Okay, Sherlock, what next?"

Blake crossed the room to sit next to her. "That was my idea. Now it's your turn."

"Well, I'm plumb out of ideas. But I did call my parents to see if they could get me in touch with my cousin, or at least my aunt."

"Any luck?"

"Dad had gone to dinner with a client and wasn't back yet. Mom thought he might have my aunt's number."

"What kind of work does your dad do?"

"Attorney. Corporate law, not the ambulance chasing kind." She grinned over at him. "And my mom stays busy with her charities and social activities. And spending my dad's money."

"Sounds like a good arrangement."

"Yeah, they're happy. How about your parents?"

"My mom works days as an administrative assistant for the Dallas County Sheriff's Department. Her nights she spends worrying about me and my sister. If more than four days pass without talking to both of us, she's convinced that something horrible has happened." Instead of annoyance, his tone was filled with affection. His gaze flicked over her. "She would like you."

Warmth filled her chest. Had he told his mother about her? Probably not. Theirs wasn't that kind of a relationship. She had mentioned him to *her* mother, but that was just to tell her about Brinks.

"What about your dad? Is he in law enforcement, too?"

"Used to be. He was killed in the line of duty when I was twelve."

"I'm sorry. That had to have been hard."

"Yeah, it was. But he was a hero. As a kid, I always wanted to be just like him."

There was a wistfulness in his tone, as if he was remembering a long-held dream that he had never been able to realize. Why did he have to be so hard on himself?

"As far as the hero part, I'd say you succeeded."

"Not hardly." He cast her a doubtful frown, but his dark eyes held underlying pain.

She studied him, trying to hear all the words he'd left unsaid. His angst wasn't just about his injury. It went deeper than that. Something happened that night that he refused to talk about.

"The guy who shot you—where is he now?"

"In prison. For a long time."

"Then I'd say you did what you set out to accomplish, and the streets are a little safer. That's my definition of a hero."

He pushed himself to his feet with a half snort and began walking toward the door. "Trust me. I'm no hero."

And she followed, frowning in exasperation.

Why did the men in her life have to hold themselves to such impossible standards?

Blake drew in a deep breath, savoring the tantalizing aromas drifting through the park. With the sun high overhead, it was a little on the warm side, but attendees of the Cedar

Key Seafood Festival were still enjoying the remnants of the cool front that had come through earlier in the week.

Tents were set up along the sidewalk bordering the park, serving everything from seafood spread to grilled shrimp to crab cakes. That was where he and Allison and Brinks currently stood—the crab cake line. It was long, but according to Allison, Thelma McCain's homemade crab cakes were worth the wait. And at two bucks each, the price couldn't be beat.

A young woman moved toward them pushing a stroller, her face lit with a contagious smile.

"Hey, girlfriend." She gave Allison a hug, then backed away. "I think we're having our best turnout ever. Mom's sold tons of her crocheted stuff."

Before Allison could respond, the stranger turned eager eyes on him. "And you must be Blake." She extended her hand and gave his an enthusiastic shake. "Darci Tucker."

"Darci owns the gift shop downtown," Allison explained. "She's also a very good friend of mine."

Blake nodded and turned his gaze back to Darci. The two women were as opposite as could be. Darci was shorter by probably a good six inches, and her hair, currently pulled up into a high ponytail that swished back and forth as she talked, was almost jet-black. And it wasn't just their looks. Where Allison was quiet and reserved, her friend projected exuberance. There likely wasn't a shy bone in her body.

Allison stepped away to squat down in front of the stroller. A chubby-cheeked little boy reclined in the shade of its cover. Blue eyes an almost exact replica of his mother's shifted to Allison, and a soft smile climbed up his cheeks.

"How's my little Jayden?"

She commenced with several sentences in baby talk. Finally, she straightened. "I can't believe he's almost a year old already."

"I know. I keep waiting to hear *mommy*, but it hasn't happened yet. Of course, I was a late talker, too, although you'd never guess it now. He's probably just waiting until he can do it right." She bent and ruffled his blond hair. "Aren't you, buddy?"

"I bet he's going to surprise us all, and his first words will be *Auntie Allison*."

Darci crinkled her nose. "That would be so unfair." She glanced down at Brinks. Although Blake held the leash, the dog was pressed up against Allison's leg. Dogs weren't normally allowed in the park, but the Cedar Key Seafood Festival seemed to be an exception.

"So who does the Doberman belong to?"

He reached down to scratch the dog behind the ears. "He's mine. But as you can see, he's gotten kind of attached to her."

That was all he would say. If she wanted Darci to know more, it would be up to her to tell her. The line moved, and he stepped forward to fill in the gap. When the two ladies had done the same, Allison glanced around her and addressed Darci, her tone hushed. "You've lived here all your life. How well did you know my cousin?"

"We weren't best buds or anything, but I knew her. Why?"

Allison lowered her voice even further. But with the hundreds of people talking all at once and the volume of the Southern rock coming from the band in the pavilion, she wasn't likely to be overheard.

"I told you about my house and boat being ransacked. Well, earlier this week, someone came in while I was sleeping and demanded that paper."

So she *had* told Darci everything. Maybe she trusted her enough to know that whatever the outcome, it wouldn't make a difference in their friendship. Or maybe she had taken his advice.

Darci drew in a shocked breath, and a dainty hand flew to her mouth. "How scary."

"I need to find out who's after that paper, and I think my cousin might know something."

"Well, if anyone would know what your cousin is up to, it would be Jasmine Porter. They used to do everything together."

"Jasmine Porter? Any relation to Vera?"

"Daughter. She's actually here today. The last I saw her, she was helping her mom man her booth."

The line moved again, and Darci took the opportunity to bid them farewell.

Blake smiled over at Allison. "Once we get these crab cakes, I'd say it's time to head back to the craft section."

They had spent a couple hours there that morning, checking out the dozens of booths that lined both sides of Second Street. If he remembered right, Allison had introduced him to Vera Porter, along with a couple dozen other people whose names he would never keep straight.

When they moved away from the crowd a few minutes later, they each held a paper tray, four crab cakes in one and a generous serving of seafood sauce in the other.

Blake dipped a crab cake into the sauce and took a bite. *Oh, yeah.* Definitely worth the wait. People in Cedar Key really knew how to cook. "So I take it you haven't had any luck getting a hold of your cousin."

Allison shook her head. "I got my aunt's

home number from my dad and left her a message. But she travels a lot, so who knows when she'll get it."

When they reached Vera's booth, a younger woman he hadn't seen before sat on a stool inside. Vera hurried around the table to clasp Allison's hand.

"I'm so glad you stopped back by. I'd like you to meet my daughter, Jasmine."

After introductions were made, Vera rested a hand on Jasmine's shoulder. "Jasmine moved to Gainesville several years ago. I'm afraid Cedar Key is too small for her."

Allison smiled. "I did the opposite, moved from the big city to Cedar Key." She cast a glance back at him. "And Blake did, too."

Of course, his move was temporary. At the thought, a hollow emptiness settled in his chest. He wasn't ready for his time in Cedar Key to end. But eventually he would have to do more with his life than hang out on his boat and stock shelves in a small-town grocery store.

"Allison is Sandra's cousin." Vera's words

cut across his thoughts. "She's even living in the old house."

Jasmine's face lit up. "Oh, cool. I have a lot of good memories of that house. Sandy and I used to be best friends."

"Used to be?" Allison asked. "Did you have a falling-out?"

"No, nothing like that. Once she left Cedar Key, we just sort of lost touch."

"Any idea why she left?"

"Who knows?" Jasmine shrugged, but her gaze dipped to the table and swept across the pieces of handmade jewelry lying there. She obviously knew more than she was willing to share.

Allison leaned toward her. "I'd love to get in touch with her."

"Sorry, I can't help you there. I've only talked to her a handful of times since she left, and the last was probably six years ago."

Blake frowned. Unless he had totally lost his ability to read people, she was telling the truth. They really *had* lost touch. But Sandra left for a reason. And this might be their only chance to learn why.

"Can we talk to you privately for a few minutes?" He wasn't concerned about Vera. But several other people milled around, looking at the items displayed on the table.

Jasmine hesitated, then shrugged and stepped out of the booth. After slipping between two of the ten-by-ten tents to the sidewalk behind, he glanced around. The area was relatively quiet. All the crowds seemed to be in the roadway. Catty-corner from where they stood was the bright yellow building that housed the Salty Needle Quilt Shop and The Gathering Place eatery. Under a picket-lined porch, several people were seated at two wooden tables having a late lunch, well out of hearing range. He kept his tone low anyway.

"Allison has had some scary things happening at her place. Her house and boat have been ransacked, and earlier this week, someone broke in during the night and held a knife to her throat. We're hoping you can help us."

Jasmine's eyes widened, worry flickering in their depths. "I'm not sure what I can do."

"Tell us what you know. Even if it seems insignificant. Sandra Morris had a house given to her. All she had to do was keep up the taxes. But she walked away and let it go for a fraction of what it was worth. Why did she leave Cedar Key? Did she learn something? Was there some family secret that she just couldn't handle?"

Jasmine snickered and gave him a rueful smile. "It wasn't anything as intriguing as that. I'm afraid it was all over a guy."

"A guy?"

"Yeah, she got hooked up with this creep of a boyfriend. He was fifteen years older than her, a total con guy. And she fell head over heels."

Blake continued to press. "You say he was a creep?"

"Through and through. I never liked him, right from the start. He made me really uneasy. He was just… I don't know, scary. But I didn't know why until it was too late."

Allison tensed beside him. "What happened? What did he do?"

"Sandy had about twenty thousand in savings and another twenty in stocks, money she had inherited from her grandparents. Bear talked her into letting him manage her assets, said he was really good with investing." She gave an unladylike snort. "He managed them, all right. Took off with all her money six months later and left her broke. Then he got himself arrested."

"Did she report any of this to the police?"

"No. She didn't want anyone to know. I think she was too ashamed. She told me, but I promised I wouldn't tell anyone. I'm only telling you because you've gotten tangled up in this mess. All that stuff you mentioned probably has something to do with Bear."

"Bear?"

"I don't know his real name. I wish I did. Sandy became a different person when he came into her life. He even got her using drugs. That's something I wouldn't have imagined in a thousand years."

Yeah, he knew all about it. He had seen too many good kids go bad because of the acquaintances they kept.

Jasmine sighed, then continued. "After he dumped her, she hung around for another six or eight months. But she was never the same.

One day she just up and left. We had contact a couple more times. Then she changed her number, and I never heard from her again."

"Do you know what he was arrested for?"

"No. Sandy just told me that he had gotten himself arrested."

"If there's anything else you remember that might help us figure out who this guy is or how we can get a hold of Sandra, can you let us know?"

"Will do." She pulled out her phone. "I'll program in both of your numbers."

As soon as they left Jasmine, Allison looked over at him, her eyes shining with respect. "Good job. I can't believe you got all that out of her."

Pride swelled in his chest, but he brushed aside her compliment. "It was just a matter of asking the right questions."

"I didn't know to *ask* the questions. How could you tell she wasn't leveling with us?" She flashed him a quick grin before he could respond. "Oh, yeah, it's your job to notice things."

They continued down the sidewalk, headed

away from the park. "How is your leg holding up?"

"I'm doing all right." But after almost five hours on his feet, his pain levels had shot way past the usual dull ache several hours ago.

"What do you say we call it a day? My feet are hurting, so your knee has to be killing you."

She was right. He would give out long before she would. That wasn't what she meant, but he couldn't deny the truth.

He shook off the negative thoughts. "So do you think this Bear is the one who hid the paper in the newel post?"

"Possibly. But why is he just now coming after it?"

"Maybe he's been in prison all this time and just got out."

She nodded. "I wish we had more to go on than a nickname. Hopefully I'll get to talk to my cousin."

As they turned onto First Street, he focused on trying not to limp. Allison's house was a few doors down. He had ridden his bike over that morning, and they had walked together to the festival. Now he wished she had met him at the park instead. With the marina a short block or two away, he would be back on his boat now, leg propped up. Even Brinks seemed to be wearing down.

When they stepped onto Allison's porch, a sheet of paper had been folded in thirds and taped to the front door.

Allison reached for the page. "Someone left me a note."

As her eyes scanned the page, her brows drew together.

Blake's chest tightened. It was either bad news from someone she cared about, or she had heard from her intruder.

She angled the sheet toward him, and his gaze dropped to the black print. It was all caps, written with a Sharpie.

Quit your snooping, or bad things will happen. I'm watching you.

Allison lifted fear-filled eyes to his. "He was there at the festival. He saw me talking to Jasmine."

A vise clamped down on his chest. She

was right. When they were standing at Vera's booth, the creep was probably not even six feet away. Wherever Allison went—on the water, around town—he was there. She was being stalked.

"Let me stay with you." The words were out of his mouth before he could stop them.

Allison shook her head. "I'm all right. I've got the alarm now. I keep it set all the time." She gave him a weak smile. "Go back to your boat and get some rest. I've got laundry to do. Then I'm going to take it easy myself. But if you want to leave him with me, I won't object." Her gaze dipped to Brinks.

"No problem." He handed her the leash, then leaned against one of the porch posts, not wanting to leave her. "What are you doing tomorrow?"

"Church in the morning."

Oh, yeah. Tomorrow was Sunday.

She smiled over at him. "You're always welcome to come."

"No thanks. I don't need to be sitting inside a church to worship God. I can worship

Him right out here, surrounded by nature."
He made a wide sweep of his arm.

"Uh-huh." She nodded slowly, her expression thoughtful. "And do you?"

"Do I what?"

"Worship God out here."

She had a point. The excuse sounded good. But no one had ever pinned him down on it before.

"Okay, you've got me. But the point is, I could. One doesn't have to be in church to talk to God."

She smiled up at him. "True."

"So what are you doing in the afternoon?"

"I haven't decided yet. Why?"

"I was thinking of coming over and using your internet, checking out arrest records for, what, nine years ago?"

She paused while she did the math in her head. "Based on when my cousin stopped paying the property taxes, nine is about right." She turned to face him and rested a hand on his forearm. "Thanks. I'm glad you're here. God sent you to Cedar Key at just the right time."

"I'm glad I'm here, too." He wasn't sure God had anything to do with it, but whatever.

She slid her hand down to give his a squeeze. "See you tomorrow, then."

He returned the gesture, then reluctantly released her. The moment she opened the door, an electronic squeal came from inside, followed by four beeps as she punched the code into the alarm panel just inside the foyer. The sounds gave him a small sense of relief. So did the sight of Brinks walking in behind her.

But he really wanted to be there himself. And if he was being totally honest, he would have to admit his desire to be with her was about more than just her protection. Because no matter how he fought it, this thing between them was developing into something much deeper than mere friendship. At least on his part.

But what about Allison? Was she starting to feel anything for him? Or was whatever she had been through in the past keeping her heart closed up tight? Was there any chance that she would eventually look at him as more than a friend?

He swung his bad leg over the bar of the bicycle and winced when he put his weight on that foot. Allison was right. His leg *was* killing him. He tried hard to hide it, to appear as strong and able as he had ever been. But she could see past it. She knew what he was.

He needed to face reality. There would never be anything more than friendship between them. Allison was physically perfect. She could probably outwalk him, outrun him and best him in a lot of areas.

If she eventually decided to risk getting into another relationship, it wouldn't be with him. Women didn't want scarred men who walked with a limp. He'd learned that a year and a half ago when his fiancée couldn't handle his injury and hooked up with his partner.

He threw a final glance at the colorful Victorian, then moved down the street, each rotation of the pedals leaving his unrealistic dreams farther behind.

Yes, it was time to accept the ugly truth.

No matter how he hoped otherwise, someone as toned and athletic as Allison would never hook up with someone like him.

EIGHT

Rain-scented gusts whipped against the sails and sent whitecapped waves breaking over the bow. Angry black clouds skidded across the sky, rolling ever closer. The sun was up there somewhere. Allison had seen it all morning.

When they headed out, the weather report promised a beautiful day with a chance of some light evening rain. What was currently barreling down on them wasn't light. And it wasn't evening. It was barely 3:00 p.m.

For the past hour, she had been trying to outrun the squall and get back to the marina. Now she was just hoping to make it to the leeward side of an island for a semiprotected place to drop anchor and wait it out.

"Is that where we're headed?" Blake held up a finger, indicating a point off the port bow. He had to shout the words over the howl of the wind. If he was afraid, he wasn't showing it. Maybe he was too macho to show fear. Or maybe he felt safe in her capable hands.

"Yeah. I'm coming into the main shipping channel and will bring us as close to Seahorse Key as I can." Unfortunately, she couldn't moor in behind it. The curve of the island would give them protection, but it was much too shallow.

She continued to guide *Tranquility* through the churning seas. In another twenty minutes, she could be back to the marina. But no way was she going to dock in this. Already the strength of the wind was generating small craft advisories. And it was getting worse.

As she neared the island, she pulled on the furling line, and the head sail slowly wrapped around the front stay. Their forward movement reduced by one half. She started the motor, then released the mainsheet. The sail slid down the mast, guided into loose folds by the lazy jacks.

Blake moved to stand beside her, steadying

himself with the rear safety line. "Anything I can do to help?"

"Nope, I've got it." She had *Tranquility* set up for single-handing, with all the lines run to the cockpit. Before she left Rhode Island, she had made sure she could handle everything without even stepping away from the helm.

As close to the northeastern tip as she dared get, she killed the motor and depressed a button marked Down. The electric windlass lowered the anchor. Once sure it was set, she secured the sail.

"How about pulling a couple of bungee cords out of that storage locker?" She pointed to the lazarette in the rear of the boat. She wouldn't bother with the sail cover. The bungee cords would secure it just fine.

With Blake's help, the task was completed in moments.

"Let's get below." Already the first fat raindrops were beginning to pelt them. She stepped around the helm, then motioned Blake down ahead of her. Brinks was already there. As soon as things had started to get rough, Blake put him in the cabin.

As she descended, both Brinks and Blake stood in the galley area looking up at her. Respect shined from Blake's eyes.

"You did well."

She closed the hatch and walked past them to sit on the long seat opposite the dining area. Blake sat next to her, and Brinks lay at their feet.

"You're a little premature in your praise. I haven't gotten us back yet."

"Well, I have full confidence in you. Your grace and competence up there inspire trust."

She snickered. She couldn't help it.

Blake cocked a brow. "What's so funny?"

"I haven't been called graceful too many times."

"Well, you are."

"You should have seen me as a kid. Total klutz."

"I find that hard to believe."

"It's true. You know all the Most Likely To awards they give out in high school? Well, I have the distinction of being named the most likely to break a limb."

Blake laughed. "That's terrible."

"Terrible, but deserved. Fortunately I've outgrown most of it." Learning to sail had done wonders for her balance. Or she just outgrew the klutziness on her own.

"Something tells me you have some very entertaining stories."

She raised her voice to be heard over the howl of the wind and the sheets of rain pelting the deck over their heads. The relentless deluge flowed over all the windows, making it impossible to see anything outside the well-lit cabin. But inside they were dry and secure.

"Yeah, I have a few."

"I don't think this is going to be letting up anytime soon. So entertain me."

She thought for a moment. "When I was in eighth grade, I got this really cool pair of platform shoes. I was so proud of them. Anyhow, I was changing classes and walking toward the cutest guy in the school. Just when I got up to him, I stepped on the edge of the sidewalk."

"Uh-oh. I think I know where this is going."

"Yep. One minute I was giving him a shy smile, hoping so bad he would notice me. The next I was sprawled out in the grass amid all my papers and books, hoping so bad he *wouldn't* notice me."

"And did he?"

"Oh, yeah, along with two teachers, thirty students and a couple of stray cats."

Blake laughed, and she laughed with him. She could joke about it now. It hadn't been so funny then, with the popular kids' mocking laughter ringing in her ears. All she could think about at the time was how her sister, Angela, would never have done something like that. Angela had always been the picture of poise and grace. Still was. But Angela would never single-hand a sailboat from Rhode Island to Florida. Or move twelve hundred miles from home to make a fresh start.

She turned in the seat so she was facing Blake. An almost imperceptible bump vibrated through the hull, as if they had brushed bottom. There were shoals nearby. But they had plenty of depth where they were anchored. Even taking into account that they were headed toward low tide. Unless they had drifted.

No, the anchor was set, and she had let out plenty of rode. She shook off the uneasiness.

"So tell me what the young Blake was like."

"Daredevil to the point of being stupid. I practically lived in the emergency room."

"What's the dumbest thing you ever did?"

"Hmm. There were so many it's hard to pick one. But I'd say sledding off the garage roof."

Allison cringed. "That sounds painful."

"The first time was great. By the time I reached the edge, I had enough momentum that I made this nice arc to the ground. Since the backyard sloped away from the house, I kept going, all the way down to the frozen creek at the back edge of our property and partway up the other side."

"I take it that wasn't Dallas."

"No, I grew up in Flagstaff, Arizona. We didn't move to Dallas until I was fifteen."

"So what happened? I'm guessing the other attempts didn't go so well."

"'Fraid not. The second time the TV antenna got in the way."

She flashed him a crooked grin. "A whole roof, and you couldn't miss one two-inch pole?"

"I was ten. What can I say?"

"So what did you break, besides the antenna?"

"The antenna fared better than I did. When the sled hit the ground, I wasn't on it. I landed on my arm, actually heard the bone snap."

A shudder shook her shoulders. "I pity your parents."

"Everyone else did, too."

She smiled over at him. Fearless as a child and fearless as an adult. Except now he channeled that courage into fighting for justice. Getting hurt didn't change that. He was still fighting for justice, in an unofficial capacity. Once a hero, always a hero.

He returned her smile, and their gazes locked. The respect she had seen earlier was still there, along with something else. A quiver settled in her stomach, accompanied by a delicious warmth. She squared her shoulders, determined to quash both. With her history, she had no business falling for anyone. But despite her best intentions, Blake was rapidly becoming more than a friend.

And he was apparently feeling it, too. He drew in a slow, deep breath, and his gaze shifted to the window. "How long do you think this is going to last?"

"Hard to say." From the time they came below, the boat had bobbed up and down in the angry waves, rising and falling, pitching and rocking. "That wind is really howling, and the rain doesn't show any signs of letting up."

She turned to look through the window at her side. Water cascaded over the Plexiglas, and in between, a mass of green hovered in the distance. Seahorse Key. She frowned. When they anchored, the island was right over the bow.

"The wind is shifting direction. It's coming out of the south now instead of the southwest."

"Is that a problem?"

"Not a big one. We're just not nearly as protected." She heaved a sigh. "At least no one seemed to be following us today."

Blake nodded, but there was hesitancy in the motion. No one was following them that they could see. He didn't say it, but she knew what he was thinking. With a mast shooting fifty-something feet into the air and huge white sails, they were much easier to spot than the powerboat.

"As soon as this—" She stopped midsentence at the *shhh* of the keel dragging through sand. She paused, waiting. There was still movement, but it had changed. Instead of bobbing freely in the water, the boat had taken up a slow, sloppy side-to-side motion.

"What's wrong?"

"The anchor dragged. We're grounded."

"Do we need to call for a tow?" The concern she would expect wasn't there. That was Blake—calm in the face of trouble.

"I don't think so. We're a couple of hours from low tide. After that, it'll come in and lift us free."

Within an hour, the storm had passed, and the sun was trying to make an appearance. She moved up on deck to assess the situation. The boat was fine, but they were a good thirty feet from where they had anchored.

She turned to look at Blake. "Given that we're stuck here for the next two or three hours, what do you say we take the dinghy to shore? Unfortunately, Brinks will have to stay. Like all the other islands here, Seahorse Key is a national wildlife refuge."

Blake stood and removed a package from one of the galley cabinets. "No problem. We'll bribe him with treats."

Moments later, they stepped from the cabin, leaving Brinks happily chewing a jerky stick. Blake followed her off the swim platform and into the small boat. After two pulls on the rope, the trolling motor sputtered to life and propelled them slowly toward the shore. It would be dark by the time they began their return trip to Cedar Key.

Blake had apparently noticed the same thing. His gaze was fixed on the western sky, where the sun was three-fourths of the way through its descent. "How are you with night sailing?"

"Good. I just follow the beacons. I know these waters so well, I think I could sail them in my sleep."

They stepped ashore where the easternmost edge of the island hooked around, and Blake pulled the dinghy onto dry ground. Then they headed down the beach, making their way along the outer curve. Waves lapped at the sand near their feet, and seagulls circled overhead, their raucous calls punctuating the gentle sounds of the seaside. Soon the light would fade, and the sky would become ablaze with color. A romantic sunset walk on the beach was so not in her plans for the day.

Blake released a contented sigh. "This is great. I missed out on this growing up. Moving to Dallas put us a little closer to the beach, but not much."

She bent to pick up a shell and turned it over in her hand. "I've spent countless hours at the beach. I grew up in Boston, then moved to Rhode Island when I got married."

"Losing your husband must have been really tough."

That was an understatement. She lost her husband when she found out he had been killed, then lost him all over again when she learned that the honest, hardworking man she had fallen in love with didn't exist.

She shrugged and dropped the shell. "It was. But you pick up the pieces, time marches forward, and each day it gets a little easier. Of course, I had a little help. I had new friends and a really supportive church family." They didn't know her past, but they welcomed her with open arms. "And my faith," she added. Which was as new as her friends were. She had Darci to thank for a lot of things.

"I'm glad it's working for you."

"What?"

"The whole religion thing."

"It can work for anybody, you know."

He picked up a piece of driftwood and tossed it down the beach. "I don't know. From everything I've seen, Christianity is just a bunch of dos and don'ts."

She frowned. "That's what a lot of people try to make it, but that's not what it is. It's all about relationships, first and foremost with God, and then with each other."

"It sounds appealing when you put it that way."

"It is."

"Maybe I'll check it out sometime."

The politely dismissive tone signaled the end of the topic. Hopefully over time he would soften. If only he could find the peace and contentment she had found before he headed back to Dallas.

Tom never did find it. If he had, their lives would have turned out differently. He would have been happy with the money he made as a cop and never gotten tangled up with the mob.

"What about you? Has there ever been a *Mrs.* Blake Townsend?"

"Almost. Once."

"Did she end it, or did you?"

"She did. Apparently active, strong law en-forcement officers are much more appealing than has-beens."

The bitterness she would expect with his

words wasn't there. What she heard instead was resignation.

She reached over to squeeze his hand. "I wouldn't know about has-beens. I see a wounded hero, someone who sacrificed his own well-being to make the world a better place. Some women find that irresistible."

He squeezed her hand in return, but instead of releasing it, entwined his fingers with hers. He stopped walking, pulling her to a halt with him.

"Thank you for saying that."

He smiled down at her, and her heart gave an answering flutter. They shared a connection, one she hadn't experienced even with Tom. They had both been wronged, both suffered. And she was having a hard time holding on to her determination to not get romantically involved. Especially with him looking at her like that. His gaze was warm, his eyes shining with appreciation.

But something else was there, too. Doubt.

"You know, that wasn't just meaningless chatter to try to make you feel better. I meant every word."

He gave her hand another squeeze then released it. She curled her fingers into her palm, holding on to the heat he had left behind. Now she had no doubt. Everything she was feeling, he was feeling it, too. And he was fighting it as hard as she was.

He resumed walking, and she fell in beside him. Up ahead and to the right, the Seahorse Key lighthouse peeked out over the tops of the palms, oaks and evergreens that covered a good bit of the island. She nodded toward the tower.

"Have you ever been to the lighthouse?"

Blake shook his head. "Is it functioning?"

"Not for the past several decades. At least not as a lighthouse. The University of Florida regularly uses the property for its Seahorse Key Marine Laboratory."

Her gaze slid away from the mass of green up ahead to the waves rolling in from the Gulf. Unease trickled over her. A shape moved toward them over the water, a boat. Although they were well into dusk, it wasn't using its running lights.

She shot a worried glance at Blake, but

he had already seen it. It moved closer then stopped, close enough to observe them, but not close enough for them to identify the captain or the type of boat.

She reached over and clutched his arm, fear crashing into her. Her voice wavered. "What do we do?"

"So far, he's just sitting there." He didn't meet her eyes. His gaze was still fixed on the water. "It may not even be the same boat."

She swallowed hard. Did Blake really believe that, or was he just trying to reassure her? She studied him for several moments. He stood in profile, jaw tight, tension radiating off him. No, he didn't believe his own words.

"We should probably get back to the boat, just in case." He turned and began walking back in the direction from which they had come. "And it wouldn't be a bad idea to stay close to the tree line. It makes us harder to see."

She swallowed hard and hurried to catch up with him. Now she wished she had the Glock. She still didn't know how to use it, but

Blake did. Friday he had given her her first lesson at the shooting range. It was clear he knew his stuff, although he never fired the weapon himself.

"Are you armed?"

"No, I'm not."

She planted her hands on her hips. "What kind of cop doesn't carry a gun?" She was only half joking.

Blake stopped so suddenly she almost bumped into him. When he spun to face her, she took a step back. Fury flared across his features, and his fists clenched at his sides. For several moments he stood motionless, brooding silence stretching between them. Then he turned on his heel and stalked away. Although his back was to her, his words reached her anyway, thrown back into her face by the ocean breeze. "One who doesn't want to risk killing the innocent."

Dread slid down her throat and settled in her gut like lead. Whatever had happened, someone had died, maybe even at his hand. Had it happened the night he was shot?

Dear Lord, help me to help him.

She hurried after him, catching up to him as he reached the dinghy. He stared straight ahead, posture stiff. The storm they had just endured was nothing compared to what was brewing behind those dark eyes.

"Do you want to talk about it?"

"No, I don't."

"It can be therapeutic, you know. Sometimes it helps to get it off your chest."

He slanted his gaze toward her, his eyes narrowed in anger. And disgust. Whether aimed at her or himself, she wasn't sure. "No, it won't help, and no, I don't want to talk about it."

As soon as she boarded, they made the short trip back to the boat in stony silence. Her question had hit a raw nerve. And she didn't know how to take it back.

Once on board *Tranquility*, Blake reached for his cell phone. "I'm calling Hunter."

"Good idea." Seeing a boat on the water didn't warrant calling nine-one-one, but Hunter could be there in his fishing boat in fifteen or twenty minutes. His presence would scare away her stalker.

And it might help diffuse some of the tension that had developed between her and Blake. They wouldn't float free for another hour. If she had to be cooped up with a sullen, brooding Blake, time would move at a snail's pace.

She slid into the U-shaped seat that wrapped the dining table and waited while he spoke with Hunter. Whatever had happened the night he was shot, she would probably never know. And there were likely plenty of other things that she would never know.

And that was okay.

She had been weakening, actually entertaining thoughts of something more than friendship with him. But today was a good wake-up call, a reminder of why she was better off alone. She needed transparency in a relationship—the complete assurance that nothing was hidden, that she wouldn't wake up one day to learn everything she had built her life on was a lie.

What she demanded was impossible.

Because everyone harbored secrets. And she wasn't ready to share hers, either.

* * *

Blake sat on the deck of his boat, feet propped up and eyes peeled for a certain white sailboat to come into view. Allison had dropped off Brinks and left the marina at nine that morning with two pot-bellied, middle-aged men. From what he had seen in the past, most of her charter customers left as soon as they docked. Not these guys. The charter ended at noon, but while she tied things off and readied *Tranquility* for her afternoon trip, they plied her with questions.

Actually, only one of them did. He apparently thought he had signed up for *Everything You Need to Know About Sailing in One Easy Class*. The other guy didn't have any questions. He came across as a know-it-all, inserting "that's right" after almost everything Allison said.

As Blake watched the exchange, he got more annoyed every passing minute. He had waited all morning to talk with Allison, and these guys were monopolizing her time. Besides that, Know-It-All seemed to be hitting on her, or at least trying hard to impress her.

When she had finished her captain duties, she walked up the dock and toward town, one on each side of her. And his plans for catching her between charters and treating her to lunch went up in smoke. She came back in the afternoon—with her next group of customers.

So he had spent the better part of the day stewing. Things had been icy between them on the sail back last night. Before they parted, she told him she would drop Brinks off in the morning, which he took to mean she didn't want him to come to her house. She was upset with him. And for good reason. Snapping at her like that was uncalled for. He owed her a big apology, if she would even accept it.

He shielded his eyes from the sinking sun and scanned the water. A powerboat cut through the waves at a good clip, probably Terrance returning from a day of fishing. Behind him, distant sails split the horizon. Brinks stood. The dog seemed to have an internal clock. Or rather a sixth sense about when it was time for the trade-off. Blake didn't try to deny it—Brinks liked him, but he adored Allison. When it came time to return to Dallas, Brinks was going to be one unhappy dog. But Brinks wasn't the only one who was going to be unhappy.

Over the next several minutes, the sailboat continued its course, and soon it became obvious. Wherever it was headed, it wasn't Cedar Key.

He heaved a disappointed sigh and moved toward the cabin. "Come on, boy." It would be better if he occupied himself elsewhere. What was the saying? *The watched pot never boils.*

Instead of following, Brinks took a longing look back.

"Come on. She'll be here soon." He scratched the dog behind the ears then gave him a pat on the back. Blake understood. This time he was as eager as the dog.

Once below, he took a drink from the cooler and picked up a book. Several minutes later, he closed it and shook his head. Mooning away all day for a woman. When had he become so pathetic?

By the time he went back up on deck,

Terrance had docked and was lounging in a pair of cutoff jeans and no shirt, his usual attire. Unless he was leaving the marina, he was always bare-chested, showing off his muscles, which were nothing to sneeze at, or the tough-guy tattoos that covered a good bit of his back, chest and arms.

Blake met his gaze and held up a hand in greeting. Instead of responding, Terrance rose and stepped into the Cuddy's small cabin. Apparently he wasn't feeling very personable. Maybe he had had a bad day fishing. Or maybe he wasn't getting work, and money was running out.

By the time Blake looked back out to sea, another set of sails had appeared. Over the next twenty minutes, the boat closed the distance until he knew for a fact that it was Allison. Brinks figured it out about the same time. His whole body grew rigid with excitement, except for that crazy right ear. It would flop forward no matter what.

Blake held tightly to the leash, watching Allison make her final approach. She stood at the helm, guiding *Tranquility* in under power, the sails already down. A young couple, probably honeymooners, sat snuggled together on one of the cockpit seats.

As she eased up to the dock, Brinks began to strain at the leash. Blake tightened his grip.

The young couple stepped off the boat and headed down the dock, arms around one another. As soon as they were out of sight, Blake released the leash. Brinks flew off the boat, down the dock and onto *Tranquility*.

Allison dropped to one knee and cupped the dog's face with both hands. "How's my boy?"

She continued her one-sided conversation, using the same tone she had used with Darci's little boy, even letting Brinks lick her cheek before she straightened.

Blake made his way down the dock. He didn't get the warm reception the dog did. Instead, she gave him a tentative smile. "Thanks for bringing him over." There was an unmistakable note of tension in her voice.

He drew in a deep breath and let it out in a sigh. He had ruined things. Hopefully he could make it right. "Can I help you with anything?"

She zipped the cover over the main sail and began to coil a line. "Thanks, but I've got it."

He nodded. "Can we talk?"

"Sure."

He glanced at Terrance. The kid had come back up on deck and sat watching them from two slips over, sipping his beer. He always had a beer in his hand but never appeared to be drunk. It seemed more of a prop, a way to look like a confident adult.

He returned his gaze to Allison. "Somewhere a little more private?" He'd rather not broadcast his relationship woes to half of Cedar Key.

"Let me finish up. Then you can ride with me. I have grocery shopping to do, so I drove the cart."

For the next several minutes, he leaned against the dock railing and watched her move about her boat. He liked watching her work. It was the way she handled herself, always competent and capable, no matter what nature threw her way.

Like yesterday. Even with the storm bearing down on them, not once had he been concerned for their safety. And when he learned they were grounded, he couldn't say he was disappointed. He could think of a lot of worse places to be than stranded on an island with Allison, walking hand in hand. Everything had been perfect. Until he got angry with her.

He followed her and Brinks to her golf cart, then slid onto the vinyl seat next to her. Brinks hopped into the back.

"Everything go okay out there?"

"No one seemed to be following me, if that's what you mean."

He cast a glance back toward the dock where Terrance sat on his boat, still watching them.

"What do you think of Terrance?"

"He's a little gruff, but he does good work. I don't think he's ever been involved in any kind of criminal activity."

"Any chance he could have anything to do with all this?"

She frowned. "I don't see how. He was here when I came, and in the past two years, he hasn't given me a minute's trouble. I don't know why he would start now."

Blake nodded. She was probably right. Terrance watching them at the dock didn't mean anything. Neither did the fact that he had a white powerboat. So did a couple dozen other people.

Allison pulled out of Cedar Cove and headed down Second Street. But instead of turning toward The Market, she continued all the way to the end to turn onto G Street. Silence stretched between them, filled with tension.

He squared his shoulders. "I'm sorry about yesterday."

She shrugged. "It's all right."

No, that was too easy. Besides, the tension between them was still there.

"No, it's not. I shouldn't have gotten angry, and I'm sorry."

"It's okay. You're forgiven." She glanced his way to offer him a weak smile. "I shouldn't have pressed. Everyone's entitled to their secrets."

He sucked in an uneasy breath. She had

said it was all right. Twice. But something had changed. The easy camaraderie had disappeared, and she had retreated behind a wall of distrust.

She turned left on Gulf Boulevard, where a sign pointed them toward the airport. Airport? He didn't know Cedar Key had an airport. At the moment, he was glad it did. He had asked for a private place to talk. This was it. There wasn't a soul in any direction, inside or outside the tall chain-link fence that bordered the short runway.

He had to make her understand. "Your question hit me wrong. I know you didn't mean it as a put-down. I guess I'm a little sensitive in that area."

Even as the words spilled out, he knew that wasn't the issue. He had closed a part of himself off from her. And that bothered her.

But he had no choice. He couldn't tell her the details of what went down that night. If he did, the respect and admiration she always had for him would be replaced with condemnation.

"I definitely didn't mean it as a put-down."

She eased to a stop and turned toward him, her gaze sincere. "You're a good cop. I have no doubt."

He looked down at his hands folded in his lap, then at the concrete runway that ran the length of the fence. Anything to avoid meeting her gaze.

Because she was studying him. He could feel it. She wasn't going to try to pry out of him what had happened that night. She wasn't even going to ask. Instead, she would stare at him, eyes silently pleading with him to let her in. If he only told her part of the story, would she be satisfied?

No. She would listen, and although she wouldn't press for further details, she would know he hadn't been totally honest with her. Those clear blue eyes seemed to look right past the walls he put up to the ugliness beneath.

He slowly lifted his gaze to meet hers, then drew in a long, deep breath. "I was doing an undercover buy. Had two detectives covering me. I'd been set up and didn't know it.

The perp pulled out a semiautomatic and started firing."

Memories surged forward, images that he had spent the past year and a half trying to erase. It hadn't worked. They were as clear as they had been the day it happened.

He shook his head. "The next several seconds were total chaos. Everything happened so fast. The perp went down. So did a twelve-year-old kid."

He squeezed his eyes shut. Those images would be indelibly etched on the canvas of his imagination until the day he died—the boy running out from around the corner, the perp grabbing him, the boy's eyes widening with horror as he clutched his stomach, and once released, his moan as he dropped to his knees and toppled face-first onto the pavement.

Blake sprang from the cart. He needed to walk. Or run. Maybe if he ran far enough, he would eventually escape the memories.

He headed down the deserted street at a brisk pace. A half minute later, Allison was beside him.

"You said there were two other detectives. That shot could have come from one of them, or even the dealer."

"It could have, but it didn't. When everything came back from ballistics, the shot that took out the kid came from my weapon." He stopped walking and turned to face her, his heart twisting in his chest. "I killed him, Allison. I killed a twelve-year-old kid."

She lifted a hand to his cheek. There was no condemnation in her gaze, just anguish for his suffering.

"It wasn't your fault. You were under fire. The kid was in the wrong place at the wrong time."

"But I killed him. If only I hadn't pulled the trigger. Or if I had hesitated. The kid would still be alive."

She gripped both of his arms and gave him a firm shake. "You couldn't hesitate. You were being shot at. You had to shoot back. To decide to do otherwise would be to lie down and die. And that's not what good cops do. They do everything in their power to take the bad guys off the street. That's what you did. Unfortunately, the kid got in the way."

"He ran out from between two buildings. The perp was right there. He grabbed him and thrust him in front of him." Nausea churned in his gut. "The coward hid behind a twelve-year-old kid."

"Then you didn't kill him. *He* did."

Blake twisted away and resumed walking. No, he wouldn't let himself off the hook that easily. It was *his* shot, *his* weapon.

"Are you hearing what I'm saying?" Allison shouted the words at his back. "You didn't kill anyone."

Moments later, she was in front of him, hands against his chest, forcing him to either stop or run her over. He stopped. She stared up at him, those beautiful blue eyes full of acceptance and understanding, and all the tension drained out of him.

"You were shooting at the person who was shooting at you." Her voice was low and soothing, but full of conviction. "The creep grabbed a kid and thrust him in the line of fire, knowing what would happen. How is that your fault?"

She paused, as if waiting for an answer. When he gave none, she continued. "It's not, so stop beating yourself up. You're taking blame that belongs to someone else."

Her hands slid upward, over his shoulders and behind his neck. "I thought you were a hero before, and this doesn't change anything. In my eyes, you'll always be a hero."

Warmth flooded him, and all he could think about was how beautiful she looked, with her hair windblown and her cheeks rosy from a day on the water, her eyes soft and pleading for him to believe her. He wrapped his arms around her waist, fighting against the longing to kiss her. She was a friend offering comfort. Nothing more. His thoughts were out of line.

Then she stood on her toes and planted a brief kiss on his lips.

And it was his undoing.

His arms tightened around her, and he pressed his mouth to hers, seeking the comfort and acceptance he craved. She gave him all he was looking for and more. She was solace from the demons of his past, a soothing balm for his tortured soul. But she offered healing for another part of him, as well—his heart. Both her words and her response to his kiss told him that she found him worthy and attractive, in spite of his physical shortcomings.

An unexpected *woof* preceded a not-so-gentle push by two front paws. He released Allison and stepped back. Her gaze met his for a brief moment, then dipped to the ground. Brinks stood at attention next to her, a mild warning in his dark eyes.

Blake gave an uneasy laugh. "Hey, you're supposed to be *my* dog."

She met his gaze with a shy smile. "You *did* give him the job of protecting me. He's just doing what he's been told."

"He's not supposed to protect you from *me*."

She bent to pet the dog before heading back toward the cart. "We might have to work on that."

He raised his brows. Did that mean she

planned on more kisses? As much as he wanted them, now that he had gotten his head back on straight, he wasn't sure that was a good idea. His motto had always been Keep It Casual. But he was having a hard time following his own creed.

He slid onto the seat, and Brinks jumped in behind him. "Thank you for listening. And for everything you said."

"And thank you for sharing. It means a lot." She started the cart and glanced over at him. "I suppose I should get you back."

He searched her eyes, trying to read what she was feeling. Regret that she had let him kiss her like that?

No, what he saw wasn't regret. More like confusion.

He felt more than a little of that himself.

There was something special developing between them. And he wanted more than anything to jump in and see where it would lead. Several scenarios ran through his mind, none of them casual.

Was he ready? Would he be willing to risk

the kind of pain he swore he would never experience again?

If not, he needed to end things here and now, drawing the line at mere friendship.

Before either of them got hurt.

NINE

Allison laced her sneakers, then pushed herself from the upholstered chair. Sunlight streamed in through the lace sheers, but Brinks didn't appear in any hurry to get up. He lay nestled into the comforter, eyes closed, chin resting on his front paws.

Last night, instead of curling up in the chair, he had stood beside her bed, staring up at her. She had even tried to coax him onto the padded seat, but he wanted no part of it. Finally, she gave in, and he jumped up on the bed to settle in at her feet.

Now it was time for him to go out. So far, he hadn't had a single accident. But she wasn't going to chance it. She clapped her hands. "Come on, boy."

Brinks opened one eye but otherwise didn't move.

"Come on, let's go for a walk."

The dog instantly perked up. *Walk* was the magic word. He jumped from the bed and hit the floor with a thud, all eagerness and puppy energy, in spite of the short night. And it *had* been a short night. Blake hadn't left until almost midnight.

The thought of Blake brought instant heat to her cheeks. What had she been thinking, kissing him like that? Worst of all, she had initiated it. She couldn't help it. He had looked so lost and alone. So...wounded.

When he opened up and bared his soul, the barrier between them crumbled. At least on her end. It wasn't until she was halfway home that her sanity returned. They were just friends. She wasn't ready for anything more. And unless she had totally misread him, he wasn't, either.

She sighed and headed down the stairs to where Brinks waited at the front door. After clipping on the leash, she followed him onto the front porch. Blake stood at the road, leaning against a light pole, phone pressed to his ear. He was dressed in gym shorts and a dry-wick shirt, the edges of his hair still damp from his workout. As she closed the door, a van drove past, hiding the soft thud, and he continued his conversation without turning.

As soon as Brinks saw him, he began pulling her in that direction. Then Blake's words drifted to her.

"I miss you, too...I know. It's only temporary. I'll be back home before you know it."

She froze. Who was he talking to? Not wanting to be caught eavesdropping, she tugged on Brinks's leash. He didn't cooperate.

A final sentence reached her before he disconnected the call. "I love you, too."

Her chest tightened, and her stomach filled with lead. Was Blake leading a double life? While he was kissing her, was there someone who was waiting for him back in Texas? A girlfriend? Maybe even a wife, despite his denial that he was married. Yet another man with secrets. Big ones. A nauseating sense of déjà vu settled over her, and she closed her eyes. *God, how could I have not known?*

Maybe it was innocent. Maybe he was talking to a family member. Regardless of who it was, the overheard conversation left her with an important realization. She was nowhere near ready to let down her guard enough to trust someone.

Blake turned to face her, lips turned upward in a relaxed smile. As soon as his eyes met hers, his smile broadened. "I didn't hear you come out."

"I'm sneaky that way."

She stepped forward, finally allowing Brinks to approach Blake, and he bent to give the dog a brisk, one-handed rub on the head and neck. His other still held the phone. Funny, he didn't look like someone who had just been caught red-handed.

He glanced at the phone and shook his head. "Moms never stop worrying, no matter how old you are. But now she can go through her day knowing one of her kids is still kicking."

Mom? He was talking to his mom? Relief swept through her, but it was tempered by reality. His stay in Cedar Key was temporary. He had just said so. Sometime soon, he would be leaving.

She forced a smile. "Worrying about her kids is a mom's job." At least *his* mom probably didn't try to push him into a relationship every time they talked. Then again, maybe she did.

His gaze slid past her toward the house, and he frowned. "Did you know you have something taped to your front door?"

She spun to look. No, she didn't know. Her attention had been on Blake when she walked out, and she had pulled the door shut without turning around. She hurried to the house, dread descending on her. In the bottom corner of the stained-glass panel was a sheet of paper folded in thirds, held in place by a single piece of tape. When she stepped onto the porch, she hesitated. Her intruder wore gloves. She knew that firsthand. But just in case...

She didn't remove the page from the door. Instead, touching just the edges, she lifted the top fold and let the bottom fold fall open. It was the same black print as before, but this time it filled the sheet. The words sent a chill sweeping over her.

I told you to quit snooping, but you didn't listen. If you know what's good for you, you'll let it go.

Wait for my instructions. Follow them to a tee. If you don't, I'll know. You can't hide anything from me. I see everything you do.

You've been warned. Twice. People who don't heed warnings meet unpleasant ends.

She swallowed the icy knot that had formed in her throat and looked up at Blake. He had apparently been reading beside her. His jaw was tight, his eyes dark with fury.

She shook her head in confusion. Last night after she and Blake had talked, Blake left Brinks at her house and took her to dinner. Then he commandeered her laptop and picked up where he left off Sunday night, searching arrest records for Levy County. Jasmine had said Sandra's boyfriend had taken off before getting himself arrested, so he might not have even had a Levy address. But it gave them somewhere to start.

She crossed her arms in front of her, suddenly feeling chilled in the damp morning air. "I don't understand. How does he know what we're doing?"

"Is your internet connection password protected?"

"It is, but the password is on the bottom of the modem. He could have copied it down when he was ransacking the house. He thought ahead enough to swap out the screws on the window latch, so I wouldn't be surprised."

Blake frowned. "For someone who knows what he's doing, it wouldn't be that difficult to hack into your computer. While I was searching arrest records, he may have been sitting nearby observing everything we were doing. And he obviously didn't like it, which tells me we're on the right track looking for Sandra's boyfriend."

"Well, if I *have* been hacked, that's easy enough to fix. I'll reset my password."

Blake took Brinks's leash from her. "I came to pick up Brinks, but I'm glad I got here when I did."

Yeah, she was, too. Somehow the threats didn't seem nearly as intimidating with

Blake at her side. "Brinks can stay, though. My charter canceled late last night. But if you want to walk him, I'll get that password changed."

By the time Blake returned from Brinks's walk, the task was done. He unclipped the leash and gave the dog a couple of pats.

"You know, we really need to call the police about the note. You should give them the other one, too."

Before she could respond, her cell phone rang. It was her aunt. The conversation began with a profuse apology for the delay in returning the call.

"I've been out of the country for the past three weeks," she explained. "I went on an African safari with three of my friends. It was a hoot. We spent several nights in a lodge where we could hear the calls of the wild animals right outside the walls. We took Jeeps through the savanna and even rode elephants."

Allison smiled. Her aunt was just as she remembered her from those two trips to Cedar Key—chatty, adventuresome and a little eccentric. She obviously wasn't sitting around feeling sorry for herself while her husband was running around with his young girlfriend.

Her aunt continued before she could comment. "But you didn't call to hear all about my gallivanting. You wanted Sandy's number."

She jotted down the number and thanked her aunt.

"You're welcome. But good luck on getting a call back. She doesn't even return my calls most of the time. Ever since Eddie, that girl hasn't been right."

Allison gripped the phone more tightly, anticipation surging through her. "Eddie?"

"She called him Bear, but I refused to. It made him sound like an animal—big and hairy."

"So Eddie was his real name?"

"Yep. I asked. Actually it was Edward, or Edwin. I can't remember which."

"Do you remember his last name?"

"No, I never asked."

She drew in a deep breath. "Do you know

about anything being kept in the newel post?" If there was some big Winchester family secret, her aunt would likely know.

"The newel post?"

"Yeah, at the house."

"The house plans were in there."

"Anything else?"

"Not that I know of."

She seemed to be telling the truth. Maybe the elder Winchesters put the paper there, and it had remained a secret until discovered by someone else. Or maybe someone else put it there, and it had nothing to do with the Winchesters.

After disconnecting the call, she dialed her cousin's phone. The outgoing message was one of those computer-generated ones. She left her name and number, then frowned at Blake.

"Now we wait. Again."

"But it sounds like we have a first name."

She nodded. "Edward. Or possibly Edwin."

"That will help narrow it down. *Bear* obviously didn't get us anywhere."

Blake followed her into the living room and

picked up the laptop. "I've got until noon. Then I've got to grab some lunch, shower, change and be at work by one."

"First day on the job." She sat on the couch next to him, still holding the phone. Next, she would call the police.

"Yep. And I won't make a very good impression if I'm late."

Two hours later, he folded the screen down with a sigh. Bobby had collected both notes, but their internet search hadn't yielded any more than it had on Sunday. An Edward Donaway had robbed a convenience store in Chiefland, and an Edward Harrison had been arrested for drunk driving. Both were too young to be Bear. The Edwins of Levy County seemed to be behaving themselves.

She walked with him to the door. "So, I guess I get to keep Brinks."

"If you don't mind. I could leave him on the boat, but six hours is a long time to be cooped up."

"I don't mind at all. He'll be happier here. Even though I did almost kick him off the bed this morning."

Blake raised his brows. "He's sleeping in your bed?"

She gave him a sheepish grin. "I know, I'm spoiling him."

"You're going to turn him into a sissy."

His tone was scolding, but there was nothing disapproving about the teasing smile he gave her.

He stepped onto the porch, then turned to face her again. The smile was gone. Instead, creases of worry made dual paths between his eyebrows. "Be careful. This latest note makes me really uneasy."

"Yeah, me, too. I'll keep the alarm set."

She watched him move down the porch steps, then closed the door. As she punched the four numbers on the key pad, the action gave her a small sense of security. If anyone came into the house, the police would be there within minutes.

That sense of security lasted through the afternoon. When her phone rang shortly after six, she snatched it from her purse. Maybe Sandra was returning her call.

Instead of a number, Unavailable stretched

across the screen. A sliver of unease shot through her as she pressed the phone to her ear. She spoke a tentative hello.

"Allison."

The voice was so raspy, it was unrecognizable. A cold knot of fear settled in her chest. He knew her number. And he knew her name.

"You don't listen well." The words were heavy with an unspoken threat.

"What do you mean?"

"You and that boyfriend of yours. You're still snooping."

"When?"

"Today."

This morning. Blake had spent two hours searching arrest records. How did the caller know?

He continued, as if he had read her mind. "I told you, I see everything you do. Now, listen carefully, because I'm only going to tell you once. There's a bulletin board in front of City Hall. Post the information there tomorrow. Do it alone, and don't tell anyone."

She strained to catch every word, not just the words but the way he said them. There was the slightest hint of the familiar. If she could just keep him talking.

"That bulletin board is behind glass. It's kept locked."

"Tomorrow's Thursday. Someone will be there to open it."

"I already told you, I don't have the paper. I gave it to the police."

"You don't have the paper, but you know what's on it. And you've been working hard to solve the code. I have to say, the library idea was brilliant. Brilliant but wrong."

Her breath whooshed out of her as if she had just been kicked. No one knew about that but Blake. Of course, no one knew about what they were doing this morning, either. Had he broken her trust? Had she taken him into her confidence, and he was blabbing it around town?

Worse yet, was he working with her stalker?

The caller didn't wait for her to gather her wits.

"Now that I have your attention, do as I say by noon tomorrow. And remember, tell no one. Cross me, and you'll find out you're playing with fire."

When he cut the connection, she sank onto the living room couch and sat staring at the phone, mind whirling. Blake had broken her trust. How could she have been so gullible, not once, but twice?

No. She laid the phone aside and squeezed her eyes shut. She couldn't have been that wrong about Blake. He was a good man— honest, honorable, selfless.

As if to confirm, Brinks dropped to a seated position in front of her and rested a paw in her lap. She cupped his face in both hands and looked into his dark eyes, searching for answers. Could the same man who willingly gave up his dog to keep her safe be colluding with a crook?

She shot to her feet. There had to be some other explanation. The caller had said he *sees* everything she does. This morning, she and Blake had sat together on the living room couch. They had Sunday night also.

And the caller had *seen* them.

The miniblinds were closed. Which left only one possibility.

She gripped the trunk of the fake ficus tree and gave it a good shake. Nothing fell out. When she ran her hands through the branches, her fingers met nothing but stems and leaves.

Her gaze shifted to the wall decor mounted over the couch—a brass-framed mirror flanked by a pair of decorative wall sconces draped with ivy. Now that she looked closely, the arrangement of the ivy on the two pieces was no longer symmetrical. The greenery on the right wound over and around the brass base and flowed naturally over the edges, relaxed and casual. But the silk vines on the left had been shifted around and bunched, as if to hide something. She pushed the greenery aside to reveal a small black box. A camera.

Shock coursed through her. The same day he'd ransacked the house, he'd installed a hidden camera. Maybe more than one.

Definitely more than one. There was one in the library, too. She had no doubt.

She sank back onto the couch, mind reeling. Her stomach churned, and she crossed her arms in front of her. She couldn't call Blake. Not on his first day on the job. But she would call Hunter. He would know what to do. The caller said not to tell anyone.

But she wasn't facing this alone. She would talk to Hunter. When Blake finished work, she would talk to him, too. They would all put their heads together. And they would come up with a plan.

She couldn't stop the smile that crept up her cheeks. Blake hadn't broken her trust.

He was every bit the hero she had always thought him to be.

Blake pedaled down Dock Street, headed for First. It didn't seem like that many hours ago that he had traveled the same route, but in the opposite direction.

He had gotten off work at seven last night, and at seven ten, his phone rang. Allison had found three cameras, one in the living room, one in the library and one in the den, each wireless. When he got to her house, Hunter and Bobby had just arrived. Bobby reported as the on-duty officer. Hunter came as a friend. After a brief search of her property, they found the accompanying digital recorder and monitor hidden in her gardening shed.

Blake shook his head. Someone was going to a lot of trouble to get his hands on that information. And that someone was more savvy than they had given him credit for. But hopefully today they would outsmart him.

Before they left Allison's last night, they had it all arranged—before daybreak, a camera would be installed across the street from City Hall, aimed at the bulletin board. It was a perfect location. One end of the building was well maintained and housed a law office. The other was vacant, the former home of Lutterloh Store, established in 1872, according to the sign above the door. The dilapidated second-floor porch offered a great vantage point for viewing City Hall, and stairs up the side of the building gave easy access.

Blake leaned his bike against Allison's porch. Moments after his knock, the door swung inward, and Allison stood framed in the opening. She gave him a friendly smile, but the usual sparkle in her eyes was gone. Tension emanated from her, and lines of fatigue were etched into her face.

"Are you all right?"

She shrugged. "I'm fine. I just didn't sleep well last night."

His heart twisted. The constant upheaval, the threats, the violation of her privacy—it was all getting to her. And he wanted nothing more than to take her away. He frowned, his mind working. He couldn't take her away permanently, but he could give her a reprieve.

"Still no charters today?"

"Nope. I have the whole day to myself."

"Then come with me."

"Where are we going?"

"I'm kidnapping you for the day."

Her smile broadened, and a bit of the sparkle returned to her eyes. "Sounds interesting. I assume Brinks is included."

"Of course. We can't leave him out."

"Is *this* okay?" She motioned at the shorts and button-up shirt she was wearing.

"It's perfect. I'm thinking of taking you

boating. My boat this time. Unless you'd rather do something else."

"Boating sounds wonderful. I'll be able to kick back and do absolutely nothing." Her smile faded, and she pulled her lower lip between her teeth. "After I post that paper."

"I'll go up there with you."

"You can't. No one is supposed to know. I have to go alone."

She was right. The note was clear. If she didn't follow his instructions to a tee, he would hurt her. Maybe he was bluffing. But Blake wasn't about to risk Allison's safety to find out.

"Then let me ride up there ahead of you. I'll go into the Artist Co-op. You won't see me, but I'll be watching you. When you get finished, head on down to the marina. I'll be right behind you."

She nodded, apparently satisfied. He'd rather stay with her, his arm draped across her shoulders, sending the message that no one was going to get to her without going through him. But watching her from the window of the Co-op was going to have to do.

"Well, if you're ready, I'll head on out." She gave another nod, and he got on his bike and pedaled away, headed toward Second Street.

After stepping inside, he wandered around, looking at the items on display. The Cedar Keyhole Artist Co-op and Gallery was a place for local artists to display and sell their work, everything from paintings to pottery to metal and wood sculpting. From the looks of things, there was a lot of talent around Cedar Key.

He glanced at his watch. Allison should be along shortly. He made his way to the front of the store and stopped at one of the two large windows. Stained-and blown-glass creations hung in front of him, glinting in the morning light. Behind them, the window offered an angled view of City Hall.

Moments later, Allison's golf cart eased to a stop. Brinks was tied off next to her. She looked around cautiously, then stepped onto the porch and disappeared inside. When she reemerged, a woman holding a set of keys followed her out and unlocked the center section of the triple board.

The woman had just relocked the glass cover when a third woman stepped onto the porch. Allison cast an uneasy glance in his direction, but there was nothing he could do. Her stalker was possibly nearby, watching to make sure she followed his instructions.

The city employee headed back inside, and the other woman leaned toward the bulletin board. Allison hurried to her golf cart. But before she could even get settled in the seat, the woman was beside her.

The conversation that followed lasted all of ten seconds. Then Allison eased away from the curb and headed down the street. Judging from the look of confusion on the woman's face, she didn't get the answer she was looking for.

Instead of following, he removed a spun glass lighthouse ornament from its hook and carried it to the cash register. His act would be a lot more convincing if he bought something.

When he reached Cedar Cove, Allison and Brinks were both waiting on her boat. He pulled a gift box from the bag he carried and handed it to her.

"Happy birthday."

She gave him a crooked grin. "My birthday's in April."

"Then Merry Christmas."

"Christmas is two months away."

"I like to be early."

She removed the lid, folded back the layers of tissue paper, then slid an index finger through the gold string, letting the ornament dangle. It was even prettier in the sunlight than it had been hanging in the window.

Her smile widened, and her eyes sparkled like the ornament. "Thank you. I love it. I always do my tree in lots of ribbon and lace and glass. So this is perfect."

After packing it back into the box, she stepped off the boat with Brinks. She didn't bring up the paper, and neither did he. He wouldn't until they were well away from the marina. There wasn't another soul in sight. Even Terrance's boat appeared deserted. But he wasn't taking any chances.

Within minutes, they were clear of the

channel, and he accelerated until he was wide-open, planing over the choppy sea. When he glanced over at Allison, she was sitting with her eyes closed, face skyward. Bringing her boating was a good idea. Nothing soothed the soul like sun on the face and wind in the hair.

He pulled back on the throttle, dropping the noise level to a dull roar.

"Who was the older lady?"

She turned her head toward him and slowly opened her eyes. "Susan Brannen, notorious gossip of Cedar Key. It'll be interesting to hear what rumors circulate on this one."

He nodded. The woman with the city had known Allison would be there to post something. Bobby was going to see to that before Allison arrived. But they hadn't made any contingencies for nosy residents.

"What did you tell her?"

"I told her that I didn't know what it meant, that I was posting it for someone else, and that was all I could say."

"Did she accept that?"

"I didn't give her a choice. I drove away."

"That was a smart thing to do, just in case he was watching."

She heaved a sigh. "Whatever my family was involved in, before it's all over, the details are going to be spread from one end of Cedar Key to the other."

He pulled back the throttle even further. They were still making forward movement, but barely. "That really bothers you, doesn't it?"

She shrugged and turned away. "I just don't like people in my business."

Yeah, she was a private person. He got that. But there was more to it than that.

"I know I told you this before, but whatever your family was involved in, that's no reflection on you. And what little I know of the people of Cedar Key, I think they'd agree."

Her lips curved up in a weak smile. "Thanks. I'm hoping you're right."

She sighed again, and the smile faded. Something else seemed to be bothering her.

"You all right?"

She crossed her arms in front of her. "When

I found that first camera, I felt sick, violated. But I was also relieved."

"Relieved?"

She nodded. "When I realized he knew about you pulling up arrest records, I wondered how he could have found out. Then he mentioned us searching the library for clues. Both of those were things that nobody knew about except you and me."

She paused and searched his eyes, as if trying to decide whether to continue. He was pretty sure he knew where the conversation was going. He should be hurt, but he wasn't.

Finally, she took a deep breath and let it out slowly. "I was so afraid I had been duped. All I could think was that you had been playing me, pretending to be my friend, all the while feeding information to my stalker."

Her eyes met his. There was sadness in their depths. "That's terrible, isn't it?"

"No, it's not. Something tells me you have good reason to doubt." He sank into the seat next to her and took her hand. "What happened, sweetheart? Who violated your trust?"

Her gaze broke from his and fluttered to

her other hand lying limp in her lap. Finally, she met his eyes.

"My husband." She drew in a deep breath. "I told you he was killed. That was the truth, just not the whole truth." She paused again, and another elongated span of silence passed.

Talking about it was obviously hard for her. Probably only a handful of people knew the story. He squeezed her hand, and she continued.

"He was murdered. Got greedy and crossed the mob. That's when I found out that everything we had built our lives on together was a lie. The honorable man I thought I had married didn't exist. He was a dirty cop owned by the mob. And I was completely clueless."

A weary sigh spilled from her mouth. "He was buying me things that should have been out of reach on a detective's pay. But he told me he had gotten a side job as a security guard. He said it paid really well." She shook her head. "I bought it hook, line and sinker."

He reached across to trace the line of her jaw with a finger. "Don't be so hard on yourself. It sounds like he was a con artist. Any other young woman in your place would have been fooled just as easily."

She turned, and her gaze slowly lifted to meet his. One side of her mouth rose almost imperceptibly. "Thanks. It's sweet of you to say so."

"I mean it. People get duped every day—people a lot older and more experienced than you were."

He eased the throttle forward, and the boat began to accelerate. When he glanced back over at Allison, she stared straight ahead, expression pensive. Two and a half years later, and she was still kicking herself.

Of course, he was a fine one to talk. When it came to regrets and not letting himself off the hook for past mistakes, he was king.

He threw the throttle all the way forward, and the bow rose. Then the boat planed off to skid along the surface of the choppy seas. Gradually, excitement replaced the sadness in her eyes, and her lips curved up in sheer enjoyment. His goal was to take her away, to help her forget, at least temporarily. If her relaxed expression was any indication, he was succeeding.

Finally, he reduced their speed. "How about a snack? I've got fruit, pretzels and cookies."

He left her to get the items and returned a minute later. She smiled up at him.

"Thanks for not being angry."

"Over what?"

"My thinking you might have something to do with what's going on."

He sat and handed her a washed apple. "No problem. Everything you learned about your husband has got to shake your trust in people."

She nodded. "People in general, men in particular."

"Well, some men can be trusted. And if you'll let me, I'd like to prove it to you. With me, what you see is what you get. No surprises."

"I'm glad." The smile she gave him lit her eyes and created a tightness in his chest. He was trying hard to rein in what he felt, to take things slow and not make any moves he would regret. The last thing he wanted to do was hurt her. But taking it slow was harder than he had anticipated. He was already dangerously close to falling for her, head over heels.

He handed her a glass of ice, then poured her some tea. For the next couple of minutes, she sipped her tea and munched on the snacks, apparently deep in thought. Finally, she broke the silence.

"Tell me a secret."

He raised his brows. "What kind of secret?"

"Anything. Something your closest friends don't know about you."

"Hmm." That wouldn't be too difficult. All he needed to do was think of something he was afraid of. Most of his close friends were guys. Guys didn't normally sit around sharing their fears.

"Okay, here's my big secret. I'm afraid of snakes. Terrified, actually. You know that Indiana Jones movie where he gets thrown into a pit of snakes? Gave me nightmares for weeks." He let an exaggerated shudder shake his shoulders.

Allison laughed. "I can sort of relate. Not with snakes, but with spiders."

He grinned at her. "So did you see the movie *Arachnophobia*?"

This time *she* gave the exaggerated shudder. "No, I'm smart enough to avoid movies like that."

"Hey, that's not fair. I didn't know the snake scene was in there."

"Okay, I'll give you that one."

He tipped his glass and downed the last of his tea. When he turned to reach for the jug, a now-familiar sight drew his gaze. A single boat bobbed up and down in the waves. Unwilling to alert its captain, he picked up the jug of tea and turned back around.

"I'm going to get something from below."

Worry flashed across her features. "Is something wrong?"

"Don't turn around, but I think our friend might be back."

Her eyes widened.

"I'm getting my binoculars. Just act normal." In his boat, they might actually have a chance of catching him.

Before stepping back into the open, he raised the binoculars. A man stared back at him through binoculars of his own. They immediately came down, the figure spun, and the boat turned and took off in the opposite direction, heading toward the Cedar Keys.

Blake set out in pursuit, bouncing over the choppy waves. The distance between them didn't shorten or grow. The boats seemed to be evenly matched for speed.

A minute later, the lead boat disappeared around the west end of Seahorse Key.

By the time Blake rounded the small island, the boat they were pursuing was nowhere to be seen. Three boats sat in the water, their occupants fishing. Two of the men he didn't know. The third he did. Terrance sat with his feet propped up on a cooler, shirtless as usual, a fishing pole in one hand and the ever-present beer in the other. He set the can down and began reeling in the line.

Blake eased to a stop next to him. A bait bucket sat at Terrance's feet, an open tackle box next to it. A towel was draped over the next seat, along with a shirt.

"Did you see a boat come by in the past few minutes?" There was no time for pleasantries.

"Yeah. The idiot screamed through here like he was headed to a fire." Each word was annoyance underlined with anger. "I yelled at him for scaring the fish away. Didn't do no good. He kept it wide-open, headed toward Atsena Otie."

Blake looked in the direction Terrance pointed. Whoever it was had apparently disappeared behind the key. And looking for wake a minute or so after the fact was pointless. The seas were too choppy.

His shouted thanks was lost under the roar of the engine as he gunned it, scaring Terrance's fish away for a second time. If he was annoyed before, he would be furious now. Blake kept his attention straight ahead. He would apologize later.

When they reached the other side of Atsena Otie Key, two more boats sat in the water. Two others made their way toward Cedar Key. One appeared to carry a family, two adults and a couple of kids. Definitely not Allison's stalker. The other was one of the local fishermen. He usually came in around this time from his early-morning jaunt out to sea. Not likely to be Allison's stalker, either.

None of the occupants of the two idle boats were able to offer anything useful. Besides the fisherman and the family, the only boat they had noticed had headed in a northeasterly direction, paralleling the keys.

Blake sighed. Following was futile. After stopping twice, they had given him too much of a lead. He looked down at Allison. "I think we lost him."

His tone was heavy with disappointment. He had wanted to give her something special—a reprieve from every reminder of the nightmare she had fallen into. He had failed.

"It's okay. Eventually we'll catch him." She reached over to squeeze his hand. "What do you say we eat our lunch at Atsena Otie? Then we can explore the island."

He nodded and turned the boat around, a sense of discouragement weighing down on him. He couldn't take Allison away from the nightmare because everywhere she went, a menacing figure was somewhere in the distance watching her. Especially on the water. They could count on it.

But predictable was good. It could be used to set a trap.

Ideas began to churn, and adrenaline pumped through his veins. Hunter had a boat. So did several other people.

Maybe it was time to enlist some help.

TEN

Darkness surrounded her. Not even the slightest sliver of light penetrated the inky blackness. She crept forward, arms extended, trying to feel her way to safety. Something waited for her. Something deadly. She couldn't see it, she couldn't hear it, and she didn't know what it was. But she could sense it. And its presence sent tendrils of fear slithering over her.

Somewhere close, a baby whimpered. The sound brought her up short. She couldn't leave it. She had to find it, get it somewhere safe. Somehow they would escape together.

The whimpering increased, growing in intensity and volume. It came from somewhere to her left, accompanied by scratching. She turned that direction and took several faltering steps. But no matter what she did, it remained out of reach.

Allison's eyes shot open, and she bolted upright with a strangled gulp. She was in her room. Moonlight trickled in through the sheers, casting patterns over everything familiar.

And there was no baby. The whining was Brinks. Instead of lying in bed with her, he was standing on his hind legs in front of the side window, scratching at the sill. His head swiveled toward her, and he gave a sharp bark, then resumed his whimpering.

She cast an uneasy glance at the bedroom door. It was still shut. Locked. If anyone was inside, that was where Brinks would be, at the door, teeth bared and hair raised. Instead, he was at the window. What did he see? Was someone trying to break in?

Brinks dropped to all fours and began to pace. The whimpering turned to a series of sharp barks that set her teeth on edge. She thrust the covers back and hurried to the window. Looking left toward the Gulf, all was well. When her gaze shifted to the right, an eerie orange glow radiated from somewhere outside her line of sight. The fear that had plagued her in her dream slammed into her full force.

Something was on fire.

She shrugged into her robe, grabbed her cell phone and ran from the room. As soon as she reached the top of the steps, she knew. An ominous orange light rose and fell, undulating behind the front door's stained-glass panel, a tortured beast doing its macabre dance.

She flew down the stairs, screaming for Brinks to follow. It wasn't necessary. He was right at her heels. As she rounded the bottom of the steps, she punched the three numbers into her cell phone. The dispatcher came on the line before she had even reached the back door.

Once finished, she disconnected the call and pulled up her contacts. There was nothing Blake could do, but he would be really upset if she waited until the next day to tell him.

While she listened through two rings, she watched the flames lick at the front of her house and prayed for help to arrive quickly.

So far, the fire seemed to be confined to the front porch. Thanks to Brinks, they would be able to save her house.

She dropped to her knees and wrapped both arms around the dog's neck, gratitude washing over her. If he hadn't been with her, by the time she woke up she could have been trapped in a burning house, with no time to escape. She pressed her face against his strong neck. "You're such a good dog."

"Allison?" Panic infused the single word. Blake was on the line, all grogginess apparently jarred from his brain.

"My house is on fire. I've already called for help, but I thought you'd want to know."

"I'll be there in five minutes."

As she ended the call, a siren screamed in the distance. It drew closer, not silencing until a fire truck had stopped in her front yard. Wade Tanner and Joe Stearn jumped from the cab and began unrolling the hose. Within minutes, all that remained of the fire was smoke and smoldering ashes...and large areas of siding and trim burned away and blackened with soot.

Her heart twisted, and her chest tightened. She had done all the painting herself, painstakingly applying each of the four contrasting colors to the intricate trim. Until an hour ago, it had been beautiful.

She sucked in a fortifying breath and squared her shoulders. Whatever damage had been done, it was repairable. She had brought the entire house back to its former glory. Redoing a front porch would be nothing.

As long as it didn't happen again. Did an electrical short cause the fire? There was an outlet on the front porch and, of course, the porch light. Maybe some wiring was faulty, arced and created a spark.

Or maybe someone set the fire, hoping to scare her into giving up information. Or worse. Would he really try to kill her?

As she mulled over the possibilities, one sentence circled through her mind—*Cross me, and you'll find out you're playing with fire.*

But she didn't cross him. She did exactly as he said.

Except for telling Hunter and Blake. And having the camera installed.

Did he find out? Did he see the camera go up? Hunter told her it had been installed before daybreak, as planned. And as of last night, no one suspicious had stopped at the bulletin board.

The ringing of her phone cut into her thoughts. She glanced at the display, expecting to see Blake's number, and instantly tensed. The number was unavailable.

She swiped the screen and put the phone to her ear.

The caller didn't wait for her to say *hello*. A hoarse voice came through the phone. "Are you ready to take me seriously now?"

"Who is this?"

It was a stupid question, one she knew would go unanswered. But her mind was spinning. There was no electrical short. No faulty wiring. The fire had been set. And all over that stupid paper.

"*You're* the one who's going to come up with answers. Not me."

"I've already given you what I have." She

tried to keep the quiver out of her voice but wasn't successful. "I posted the paper just like you told me."

"You also had a camera installed. I should kill you for that. You're lucky all you got out of it was a house fire. Now give me the numbers before something worse happens."

Her shoulders sagged. He had won. Actually, he had won from the first moment he stepped foot in her house. Because ever since then, she had lived in fear, her serenity robbed. And she had gained nothing. Eight or ten sharp minds working on those numbers, and not one of them had been able to crack the code.

She heaved a sigh. Let him have the numbers. She didn't care anymore. Her life was more important than whatever was out there. "45, 87, 45, 165, 255 and 282."

"That's not it." Cold fury underlined the words.

"Yes, it is. I swear it is." Why didn't he believe her?

"You're lying."

"No, I'm not. Those are the numbers." She

squeezed her eyes shut and called up the image. It would be forever embedded in her mind's eye.

Her eyes shot open. "No, wait. There are letters, too. R45, 87, G45, 165, R255, 282."

"You're still lying. How about a bomb under your bed next time? Or I could finish what I started when I had the knife at your throat."

Panic pounded up her spine and swirled through her brain, scattering her thoughts in a thousand directions. How could she convince him that she was telling the truth?

"I'll get the paper. I'll ask for it back from the police."

He responded with an irreverent snort. "And try to set another trap? I'll pass." His tone was thick with sarcasm. "You think you outsmarted me, finding those cameras I planted. But I'm still watching. There's only one way you're going to be rid of me. Give me what I'm asking for."

"I already have." She put some force behind the words, in spite of the band of panic constricting her throat. "That's it. That's everything on that paper." She could see it as clearly as the night she discovered it. "Wait, there's a point. The 255 is 2.55."

Another snort. "You think I'll be satisfied getting it piecemeal? Look, I'm running out of time. Which means *you're* running out of time. Give me the *whole* thing. Now."

"That *is* the whole thing. There's nothing else."

"Fine. We'll do it the hard way. I'm coming for you, and you're going to lead me to what I'm after."

The phone went silent, and cold terror gripped her, along with a sense of helplessness. No matter what he did to her, she couldn't produce something she didn't have.

Her gaze traveled up the road and met a familiar figure on a rickety old bike. Relief washed through her. Suddenly she wanted nothing more than to throw herself into the safety of his arms and stay there forever. She corralled the urge and stood motionless, watching him approach. She was a strong, independent woman. She wasn't going to act like a weak-kneed halfwit.

As soon as he reached her yard, Blake stepped off the bike and let it fall over. He reached her in three long strides. The next moment she was in his arms, her face buried against his neck, sobs threatening to claw their way up her throat. She gulped in several breaths and swallowed hard, determined not to break down.

And Blake just held her, instinctively knowing what she needed, which endeared him to her even further. Finally, she released her hold on him and stepped back.

"It was him. He called and said he set the fire. It was retribution for our having the camera installed."

"You could have been killed." His eyes darkened with fury, and he began to pace, agitated gestures punctuating his words. "The whole house could have gone up in flames, and you would have been trapped on the second floor."

"It could have, but it didn't." She rested a soothing hand on his arm, her tone low. "Brinks woke me up."

"Thank God."

"I have, believe me."

He stopped pacing to stare at her. That clearly wasn't what he meant. A smile slowly climbed up his cheeks. "Then maybe I should, too. Someone was watching out for you." He cast a glance at where Wade and Joe were rolling up their hose. "Have you told them it wasn't accidental?"

"Not yet. I had just finished the call when you got here."

She made her way over to where the two men were working. Wade cast a glance at Blake, then offered her a sympathetic smile.

"Sorry about all this." He tilted his head toward her porch. "Don't start any clean-up until we're finished with our investigation."

She nodded in agreement. "The fire was set."

Wade's eyes widened. "Are you sure?"

"Positive. He just called. Said it was a warning."

"Who?"

"I don't know. But he's been stalking me."

Wade frowned. "The investigator will be

in touch with you in a few hours to take your statement. Are you up to it?"

"I will be."

Blake draped an arm across her shoulder and led her toward the side of the house. When she reentered, she would have to use the back door. The porch was no longer safe.

He drew her to a stop, concern still etched in his features. "I assume you gave the caller what he wanted?"

"I did, but he kept insisting that I was keeping something from him."

"So he'll be back."

"That was a promise. He said he's coming back for me and going to force me to lead him to what he wants."

Blake grasped both of her hands, a sense of urgency radiating from him. "You need to go somewhere safe. How about staying with Darci for a while, just until we catch this guy?"

She shook her head. "I would never put Darci or her sweet little boy in danger."

"Then let me at least put you up at one of the motels in town."

What? Give up the home that she had put so much work into for a single motel room, guests on either side? She must be losing her mind, because the idea actually had appeal. Her warm, cozy home had become cold and terrifying.

"All right." She gave a brief nod, and all the tension seemed to drain from Blake. "But I pay my own way."

"Agreed." He looked at his watch. "It's only three thirty. If you want to get a little more sleep, I'll stand guard downstairs."

She smiled up at him, her heart fluttering in her chest. He was making himself her own personal bodyguard, her knight in shining armor. And it was wreaking havoc with her emotions. He would probably stay to protect her until whoever threatened her was securely locked up. Then he would head back to Dallas and resume his life. Unfortunately, by then she was going to be hopelessly in love.

"Thanks, but I'm up now. I don't think I'd be able to go back to sleep. But if you want to hang out, I won't be opposed. We can see what kind of lineup early-morning cable offers."

"Probably not great, but it's worth a try. Then after daybreak, we'll work on getting us both rooms."

"Both?"

"Wherever you are, I'm going to be right next door."

His words and the care behind them sent tears once again surging too close to the surface. The strain of the night's events was wearing on her.

She drew in a stabilizing breath. "What about Brinks?"

He frowned. "Most places don't allow pets. Maybe we can find someone who will keep him, just at night. Darci?"

"She's a definite possibility. I'll check with her." Darci didn't mind dogs. And a furry buddy wouldn't be a bad thing for Jayden, either.

She reached down to stroke Brinks's head. He hadn't left her side since she emerged from the house.

"I hate to think about what would have

happened if he hadn't woken me up when he did. He very possibly saved my life." She gave Blake a weak smile. "When you leave, I might not let you take him."

"Then I might just have to stay."

Her stomach did a somersault and settled into a quivery lump. Was he really thinking about staying? "What about your life in Dallas?"

He shrugged. "I have a life in Cedar Key now."

"But you have family and longtime friends in Dallas."

"They can visit us in Cedar Key."

Her head was swimming. Had he just said *us*? As in the two of them, a permanent couple?

No, she was making more of it than warranted. They were friends, nothing more. He had kissed her the one time, next to the airport. But it was in a moment of high emotion. And it hadn't happened since. He had been burned and wasn't interested in anything permanent. He had all but said so.

Her eyes met his, and what she saw there

blew that theory to pieces. The warmth in his gaze conjured up images of much more than mere friendship. He lifted a hand and cupped her cheek, then slid it back to lace his fingers through her hair. She closed her eyes and leaned into his touch.

His words washed over her, soft but filled with meaning. "I came to Cedar Key looking for some direction in my life. I had no intention of staying. But now that I'm here, I don't want to leave. I feel as though we're on the verge of finding something special. I'd like to at least explore what that is, if you're willing."

Her heart pounded, and she suddenly felt light-headed, as if his mere presence had sucked all the oxygen from the air. He was right. They did share something special. She had felt it almost from the start.

Was she willing to give it a try? Could she let down her guard enough to trust him with her heart?

She opened her eyes and dipped her head. It was such a small movement, but with that simple little nod, she was embarking on a new phase of her life.

Never had she been so excited and terrified at the same time.

Blake gripped the metal handle on the glass door and hesitated before swinging it open. There was nothing to be uneasy about. It wasn't like he would be walking into a room full of strangers. He was well acquainted with at least a third of the people there.

It was just that, except for weddings and funerals, he hadn't stepped foot inside a church in over sixteen years. Nothing from past experience did anything to draw him back. What he remembered was a long list of rules, standards he could never hope to attain. And the strong sense that he didn't belong—that he wasn't worthy, and everybody knew it.

But he was doing this for Allison. Church was an important part of her life, her faith an integral part of who she was. He needed to at least check it out.

Or maybe he was doing it for himself. An itchy dissatisfaction had dogged him for the past eighteen months, growing with each passing week. Maybe it was there even before his accident, that nagging voice that prodded him to always go for the dangerous assignments, the increasingly risky sports, forever asking *Is this all there is?*

Was the answer inside those four walls? Was there something he had missed during his rebellious teen years, something that would give his life meaning and bring him the same sense of contentment that Allison obviously experienced?

He pulled the door open, and music washed over him, a guitar, keyboard and drums. Several people stood in the entry area, exchanging hugs and conversing quietly. Across the crowded space, Hunter turned then closed the distance between them.

"Welcome." A firm handshake accompanied the greeting. "If you don't already have a seat picked out, you're welcome to sit with me. Allison's up front, but she'll join us when worship is over."

Blake followed Hunter into the sanctuary, down the center aisle to the third row from the front. His eyes immediately sought out Allison. As Hunter said, she was already on the platform, sitting next to Darci. Her eyes were closed, and her face reflected serenity. Wherever her mind had taken her, it was light-years away from the stress of her daily life.

Her eyes opened, and the moment they met his, a smile climbed up her cheeks, adding joy to the serenity already on her face. If he had any doubts about whether he should be there, her expression laid them to rest.

With four beats on the drum set, the music changed, and everyone in the building stood. Song lyrics appeared on a screen at the front. Throughout the piece, Allison cast several glances his way, silently telling him she was glad he had come. Words flowed from her mouth, perfectly blending with the other voices so he couldn't pick hers out. He wished he could. Somehow he knew it would be sweet, haunting, filled with meaning from the deep well of emotion she carried within.

The band segued into the next song, a slow, worshipful number, and soon she seemed to not be aware of him at all. Her head was tilted back, eyes raised heavenward and face shining with adoration. She was onstage, but she wasn't performing, at least not for the people sitting in the pews. Instead, she was in her own private place, singing for an audience of One. As Blake watched her, he was struck with the sudden sense that he was eavesdropping on something sacred.

New words appeared on the screen, and the drums and guitar fell silent, leaving only the keyboard. A single female voice joined the tinkling melody, and he was immediately drawn in. Her voice was every bit as beautiful as he had imagined—clear, sweet and fluid. It wrapped around him, touching something deep inside.

But it wasn't just the quality of her voice. It was the words and the way she sang them. *"Draw me close to you"* was a heartfelt plea. When she sang *"never let me go,"* she meant it. Allison's God wasn't the distant, frightening God of his childhood, looking on with judgment. He was a loving father, protector and friend. It was no wonder she clung to her faith—when she came to God, she found comfort rather than condemnation.

When the service was over, they made their way down the aisle and out the doors while most of the congregation greeted them.

She turned to face him at the golf cart. "So what did you think?"

"Not what I remembered."

"Is that good or bad?"

"Good."

"So dare I hope you might be a repeat visitor?"

"That's a pretty safe assumption." He couldn't say he found what he was looking for. But today was a good start.

He settled into the golf cart next to her. "Where to now?"

"Lunch." She heaved a sigh. "I'm so ready to get back into my big, fully stocked kitchen." Harbour Master Suites' Sea Pearl had a more complete kitchen, but it was booked. "I know it's only been three days, but if I have to eat one more microwaved dinner, I'm afraid you're going to see the mean side of Allison."

"I don't think Allison has a mean side."

She cocked a brow at him and began to back out of the parking space. "You haven't seen me when I've been snowed in and denied sunshine and fresh air for several days."

He laughed. "In that case, what do you say we go make lunch at your place?" As long as he was with her, she would be safe.

After the fire, he had considered staying at the house and sleeping on her couch. But with two floors and windows in every room, it was too hard to secure. So they had headed to Harbour Master Suites and booked Tropical Tranquility and Corrigan's Reef, the only two rooms with an interconnecting door.

Now for the first time since meeting her, he was resting easy. Her stalker would have to be crazy to try to accost her, with him right next door. Armed with a pink Glock. Not exactly a he-man's weapon. But he didn't own a gun anymore, and Allison didn't know how to use the one she had.

So having him take possession of it made total sense. Using it would be a last resort.

But if it came down to the creep's life or Allison's, he wouldn't hesitate.

As they pulled into Allison's driveway, her cell phone rang. She glanced at the screen, and her eyes lit with excitement.

"It's Sandra."

As Allison talked, his heart began to thud. After the fire, she had left her cousin a second, even more urgent message. It had apparently worked. Sandra was talking, evidently not holding anything back.

Finally, Allison touched the screen and dropped her phone into her purse. "I got a name, date of birth, description, you name it. But it doesn't sound like he's our guy."

"Why do you say that?"

"The height and build doesn't fit the guy who came into my room. He was muscular but not huge. According to Sandra, her boyfriend was built like a linebacker for the Tampa Bay Bucs."

"Maybe he's lost weight, slimmed down over the years. They probably weren't feeding him in prison like he was accustomed to."

She stepped from the cart and headed

around back, bypassing the front porch. It looked like it had the night of the fire, with the addition of yellow caution tape. According to Allison, the insurance adjuster had been out, and she had contacted a couple of contractors for estimates.

He followed her into the kitchen and locked the door behind him. "So what else did you learn?"

"His name's Edward Stevens, birth date September 27. If her math is correct, he was born in 1968, but it wouldn't hurt to go a year or two to either side."

"Anything else?"

"About five-ten, dark hair, dark eyes. Some pretty impressive tattoos—an eagle in flight spanning his chest, a busty woman wrapped in an American flag on his right arm, and several others." She pulled some hamburger from the freezer and prepared to defrost it. "Of course, the guy who came into my room was wearing long sleeves, so I wouldn't have seen any tattoos."

"What did she say he was in for?"

"Drug charges and second-degree murder."

"Did she say what kind of sentence he got?"

"She didn't know. He drained her bank accounts and took off a week before he got arrested. Then he sent her a letter, trying to act all lovey-dovey. She wrote him back and told him she hoped he rotted in prison."

"Smart girl. Does she know of anything he might have hidden?"

"No, she doesn't, but she said it wouldn't surprise her."

He pulled out his phone and started to scroll through his contacts.

"Who are you calling?"

"My former supervisor back in Dallas. I'm going to see what he can find out." He owed him a phone call anyway. Doug called regularly to check on him and, during the months following his injury, showed the most concern of anyone, next to his family. His friends started out that way, but their phone calls got fewer and further between. His partner, of course, avoided him like the plague.

Allison nodded. "Good idea. We'll put Cedar Key on it, too."

When Doug answered, his voice held an

undertone of pleased surprise. Usually he was the one who initiated the calls instead of the other way around.

"So how's Cedar Key treating you?"

"I can't complain. I spend my days fishing, working out in the gym, hanging around town and visiting with the folks here. I've gotten a part-time job at a grocery store to help keep me out of trouble."

"Well, you sound good, my man. It must be agreeing with you."

"It is. Friendly people, clean salt air, laid-back way of life. You can't beat it." He glanced at Allison, who stood at the stove, her back to him, browning hamburger for spaghetti sauce. "I even went to church this morning."

"Whoa, Cedar Key *is* turning your life upside down. I'm happy for you."

"I need a favor, though. I need to find out everything I can about a guy named Edward Stevens. There's a lady here who's being stalked, and we think he might have something to do with it."

Doug's easy laughter flowed through the

phone. "I should have known there'd be a woman behind your sudden cheeriness."

Though the comment begged an answer, he let it pass. Doug would love to know where things with Allison were headed. But he couldn't fill in his former supervisor until he figured it out himself.

"I've got stats, if you're ready to take them down."

When Doug indicated he was, Blake gave him what Allison had relayed.

"I'll get right on it and let you know what I learn."

"Thanks. So how is everyone back at the department?"

"Good. Dawson's wife finally talked him into retiring, Stanger's engaged and Peterson's wife just had twins." He paused, and when he finally resumed speaking, a bit of the joviality had left his voice. "Felicia and Rick are no longer together. She left him for some guy who plays guitar in an amateur rock band. They're currently off on a rock climbing expedition."

Blake stood gripping the phone, waiting for

that sense of triumph to sweep over him, or at the least, satisfaction that although he no longer had her, Rick didn't, either. Instead, he felt nothing at all.

He turned to watch Allison remove a jar of spaghetti sauce and a can of mushrooms from the pantry, then make her way back to the counter. She was still dressed from church, her golden hair falling in waves around her shoulders. Her dress reached a point just below her knees, some lightweight fabric that fluttered as she moved. She was strong and independent, but sweet and feminine at the same time.

And he silently thanked God that Felicia had left him and he had grown so dissatisfied with his life. And he thanked Him for all the events that brought him to Cedar Key, even his accident. Because if it hadn't been for that, he would still be searching for meaning, chasing the next thrill.

"Are you okay?" Doug's words reminded him of the long span of silence that had passed. "I thought you'd want to know."

"Yes, I'm fine." He cast another glance at

Allison. "Better than fine. I'm sorry for Rick. And I hope Felicia finds what she's looking for."

After disconnecting the call, he crossed the kitchen to where Allison was dropping pasta into boiling water. He stood for several moments, then stepped forward to wrap his arms around her waist and plant a kiss on the side of her neck.

She laid down the wooden spoon she was holding and swiveled her head to bring him into her peripheral vision. "What was that all about?"

"Thank you."

"For what?"

"For everything."

She turned until she fully faced him and wrapped both arms around his neck.

"*I* should be thanking *you*. I haven't done anything."

"Yes, you have. You've made me feel welcome right from the start. You've taken me under your wing and incorporated me into Cedar Key life. And you've led me to the peace and contentment that I came here to find."

He couldn't tell her about the rush of emotion he had felt watching her cooking for him. Or how his heart picked up every time he looked at her. Or how the softness in her gaze at that moment was spurring thoughts of forever.

At least not yet. They had a lot of exploring to do. And he had his own tangled thoughts to deal with.

Before his injury, he had played as hard as he worked. He and his friends did all kinds of extreme sports—skiing, rock climbing, bungee jumping. The more exciting, the better. And Felicia had been right in there with them.

After his injury, his friends tried to keep in touch, but he was deadweight. With a knee made of metal alloys and a leg riddled with bullets, he was relegated to sitting on the couch. And his friends weren't the card-playing, movie-watching type. Neither was Felicia. If they had stayed together, she would have resented him for holding her back.

Of course, Allison was in the same great shape. If he made this thing with her permanent, would she eventually feel the same as Felicia? Would she one day think of him as deadweight? A noose around her neck?

His arms tightened around her slender body, and she responded by pressing her face against the side of his neck and holding him even more tightly.

No, she wouldn't eventually feel the same as Felicia. She knew everything about him— his disabilities, his hidden insecurities, even the ugly details of what happened that night. And she still accepted him. And cared for him. Maybe even loved him.

No, Allison wasn't Felicia.

Not by any stretch of the imagination.

ELEVEN

Allison stood in the darkened kitchenette, downing a glass of water. She wasn't really thirsty. More like restless. Something had awoken her, and she couldn't even say what.

She put the glass in the sink and leaned back against the counter. Soft gray light seeped in through the large windows, not quite reaching the corners of the suite. Silence draped everything, inside and out.

She pushed herself away from the counter and crossed the room, her nightgown swishing softly around her legs. The bedside clock said 3:17 a.m. Its red numerals glowed eerily in the darkness. Uneasiness crawled along her skin.

What was wrong with her? The first three nights she had slept like a log, even without Brinks next to her. Since pets couldn't stay at Harbour Master Suites, Darci was acting as surrogate parent for the time being.

But even without Brinks, she still felt secure. Blake was in the next room. A couple of raps on the wall would have him at her door in ten seconds flat. Besides, there were only two ways in, three counting the interconnecting door. No one would be likely to break in the front; there was too much of a chance of being seen. To come in the side, he would have to get past Blake.

And the back wasn't an option. A good portion of the Harbour Master Suites was built over the water, resting on pilings rising out of the Gulf. Her balcony was a good twelve feet up. No one was coming in that way unless he could fly.

She moved to the table and sank into one of the chairs, breathing in the tranquility of the room. She was pleased with the accommodations they had chosen. Airy and open and decorated in soft blues and whites, the suite offered the soothing atmosphere she needed. Outside the large windows was an unbroken view of the Gulf. Currently, clouds obscured all but the brightest stars, and far below, silver-tipped ripples danced in the moonlight. The moon wasn't visible from inside the room, but she had seen it earlier, a gleaming crescent suspended against a blanket of black velvet.

Her gaze slid farther right, and she drew her brows together. All the way around the balcony was wooden railing painted a cheery blue, each four-by-four post topped with a painted wooden finial. But something was wrong. Midway between two finials where there should have been smooth, flat rail was an object, slim and curved. It wasn't there earlier. Each evening, she and Blake sat out there talking, watching the sky deepen from navy to black.

She rose from the chair, planning to click on the balcony light. Before she could turn, movement caught her eye, a shadowed form rising behind the pickets. She stood frozen in place as one gloved hand, then another, clasped the top of the railing. Finally, a head appeared, wearing the now-familiar knit ski mask. Her heart leaped into her throat, and she gasped and stumbled backward.

The next moment, the head dipped below the railing, and both hands disappeared. He had seen her. And he was getting away.

She hurried to the door, flipped the light switch and stepped onto the L-shaped balcony that wrapped the room. A low sputter reached her, an outboard on idle. She rounded the corner and ran that direction. Occupying the same spot on the railing was the object she had seen earlier—a grappling hook. The sense of security she had enjoyed for the past three days shattered into a thousand pieces.

The sputter became a roar, and a boat shot into the night, a single occupant at its wheel. She leaned forward, straining to see something identifiable. But with the darkness of the night and the balcony light behind her, it was hopeless.

She came back inside and rapped on the connecting door. Moments later, it swung open, and anxious eyes swept her up and down. She rushed to assure him.

"I'm all right. But I think you need to look at this."

She led him out the door and down the length of the balcony, then leaned over the rail. A rope dangled from the eye of the grappling hook, its other end submerged, slipping back and forth with the movement of the sea. Something else floated nearby, a tangled mass of rope and wood.

She pointed at the object. "What is that?"

Blake frowned, deepening the vertical lines between his brows. "I believe it's a rope ladder."

"He must have dropped it on his hurried trip back down."

He stepped away from the rail. "We need to call the police. If they can retrieve that ladder, maybe they can find out where it was purchased. That could lead us to the perp."

It was worth a shot. Everything else they'd tried had failed. And it wasn't for lack of effort. Everyone was on high alert. Everywhere she went, someone had her back, watching from afar, hoping to see something suspicious. Hunter was doing triple time, keeping up his schedule with Cedar Key PD and following her charters every chance he got. And several other boat owners had pitched in. Even Terrance had taken a turn and made a trip out on the water when neither Hunter nor Blake was available. A weary sigh escaped her. Something needed to break soon. She couldn't afford to keep up this lifestyle forever. And Blake probably couldn't, either.

She followed him back inside and picked up her phone. Once finished with the call, she joined him at the kitchen table.

He reached across to take her hand. "You doing okay?"

"I'm fine. I'm just trying to not think about what would have happened if I hadn't woken up when I did." She swallowed hard.

"Yeah, me, too." He drew in a deep breath and let it out slowly. "I haven't heard back from Doug, but Hunter called me."

He did? Why hadn't Blake told her?

He answered her unspoken question. "He

called late last night, right after you had gone to bed. I figured I'd wait till this morning to tell you."

"Did he learn anything interesting?"

"Yeah, he did. Bear Stevens is still in prison and not likely to get out anytime soon. He got sentenced to life, and he's just exhausted his last appeal."

Allison nodded. "It sounds like he's definitely not our guy."

"Unless he's directing it from prison."

"But why bother? I mean, if he does have something hidden out there, it's not going to benefit him now. Not where he's spending the next thirty or forty years."

"You have a point." Blake stood and walked toward the door. "The police should be pulling up any minute."

Allison followed him from the room. "You know, there's one thing about all this that doesn't make sense. Why was he carrying a rope ladder? He already had the grappling hook with the rope, and he obviously had no trouble scaling it."

Blake stopped and turned to face her, his jaw tight, his posture stiff. The moment his eyes met hers, a cold knot of fear filled her stomach.

"The ladder wasn't for him." His tone was ominous, his gaze penetrating. "It was for you."

Blake slid tomato wedges from a cutting board into a bowl containing a variety of greens. Pleasant aromas wafted from the oven, some kind of a chicken casserole that he had helped Allison put together. The digital timer counted down the minutes, while a small television droned on, airing the six o'clock news from its place on the end of the counter. Brinks, full and happy, lay in the corner next to his licked-clean dish.

Blake drew in a fragrant breath. Their sixth home-cooked meal in six days. He could get used to this. Actually, there were a lot of things about Allison that he could get used to. And a lot he didn't want to live without.

Allison plopped some cut-up cucumber into the bowl and set to work grating a carrot. When finished, she leaned back against the counter and frowned. "How long are we going to have to keep this up?"

He wrapped his arms around her and pulled her to him. "Hopefully for a long time. I'm kind of enjoying spending almost every waking minute with you."

She gave him a gentle push and twisted out of his arms to pace the kitchen. "That's not what I mean. For the past seven nights, I've been paying to stay at the Harbour Master Suites while my house sits empty a few blocks away."

He knew what she meant, but it was a discussion he didn't want to have. Even though he had been thinking the same thing.

She stopped pacing and continued. "So far, the only thing we have is a rope ladder, and the chances of that leading anywhere are slim to none."

Blake sighed. She was right. None of the local stores carried that particular model, even on the mainland. So it had likely been bought online. Cedar Key PD was currently working on seeing what they could find out through Amazon.com, but it was a long shot.

"Let's give it a few more days." Eventually she *would* have to move back home. But he wanted to put it off as long as possible. When that time came, he would enlist the help of every officer Cedar Key could spare.

Allison closed the distance between them and again stepped into the circle of his arms. "All right. A few more days." She smiled up at him. "So tell me another secret."

"Huh?"

"You're scared of snakes. What else don't your closest friends know about you?"

"You like this 'Tell me a secret' game, don't you?" He hugged her more tightly. After all she had been through, she wanted to make sure she knew everything about him. And he was okay with that.

"Well, I sometimes get choked up during sad movies."

Her smile widened. "Nothing wrong with that. I can cry over McDonald's commercials."

"That's pathetic."

"No, it's not. The soldier comes home from

Afghanistan, and his family takes him to McDonald's for a Big Mac and fries. It's touching."

Yeah, he could see that. And he could see Allison thinking so. That was one of the things he loved about her, her sensitivity. He matched her smile with one of his own. "If you say so."

She dropped her arms and nodded toward the timer on the oven. "Five more minutes. Shall we get the table set?"

He released her and turned to remove two plates from the cupboard. His gaze shifted to the television screen where a colored band across the bottom announced a breaking news story. Even with the low volume, three words drew his attention—*Prison break, Starke.* Starke was two hours from Cedar Key.

When Allison started to speak, he held up a hand to silence her. Her gaze followed his to the screen, and she hurried to turn up the volume. A somber reporter stood in front of a white stone structure, dusk settling around him. The camera panned out, and another stone structure came into view, the two connected by an arch bearing the words Florida State Prison.

An hour earlier, two inmates had escaped. But not before killing two guards and leaving a third in critical condition. The name of the first prisoner meant nothing to him. It was some guy serving a life sentence for killing his ex-wife. When the reporter gave the name of the second, his blood froze in his veins. Edward "Bear" Stevens, serving a life sentence for second-degree murder related to a drug deal gone bad.

He turned at Allison's sharp intake of air. The blood had drained from her face, and she suddenly looked on the verge of collapse.

"It's him." Her voice was paper-thin, her blue eyes wide. "He's behind everything that's happening."

He pulled her firmly against his side. "Not necessarily. Stevens's escape from prison could be coincidental." His tone lacked conviction. Ninety-nine to one, she was right.

She pulled her lower lip between her teeth

and shook her head. Deep creases marked the space between her brows. "It's no coincidence. He mentioned he's running out of time."

"Who? When?"

"My stalker, the night of the fire. When he called, he said, 'I'm running out of time, which means you're running out of time.' I think Bear Stevens is the one who hid the paper. Even though he's been in prison for the past nine years, he's had someone on the outside working for him."

Blake's gut tightened with every word out of her mouth. He continued her line of thought, picking up where she had left off. "He knew he was going to be out soon, one way or another. Plan A was to get his conviction overturned. When that didn't work, he decided to implement Plan B."

Allison lifted fear-filled eyes to meet his. "And now he wants whatever he hid nine years ago. And he needs that paper to find it."

"Which means we need to stay at the Harbour Master a little longer. It's too hard to protect you here." He glanced around him, uneasiness sifting over him. The doors were locked. So were all the windows. But that wouldn't keep out someone who really wanted to get in.

The oven timer began to emit its persistent beeps. Allison pressed the button then reached for two oven mitts. "Let's take this back to the hotel."

"Good idea." He was going to suggest the same thing. What had seemed perfectly safe ten minutes ago had suddenly become more of a risk than he was willing to take. In fact, nothing seemed safe short of keeping her shut up at the Harbour Master, surrounded by Cedar Key's finest.

"What's your schedule for tomorrow? Any charters?"

"One in the morning and one in the late afternoon, early evening."

His chest clenched. "Early evening?"

"My sunset sail. It's popular with the honeymooners. We head out at five and come back at seven. At least till daylight savings time ends this Sunday. Then it'll be four to six."

He frowned. "It'll be dark when you get back."

"Not totally, but almost."

He would stick close by on both. He wasn't working at The Market tomorrow, so he hadn't asked anyone for help. For the morning charter, he would man the boat with her. For the evening one…well, honeymooners probably wouldn't want an extra person tagging along. So he would follow at a distance, closing the gap as night drew nearer.

Allison put the hot casserole dish into its basket and sealed the salad bowl with some plastic wrap. As he waited for her to relock the back door, he held tightly to Brinks's leash, eyes scanning the darkness. Nothing drew his attention. There was no sign of movement, no sound other than waves breaking a short distance away. Even Brinks appeared unconcerned, which offered some measure of comfort. Brinks had turned out to be more of a guard dog than he had given him credit for.

He settled into the golf cart next to Allison, the casserole between them, the salad in his lap and Brinks in the back. Allison turned the key and slanted a glance at him.

"You know, it sounds crazy, but I'm almost relieved."

She pulled out onto First Street, and he waited for her to continue.

"I'm uneasy. Actually, I'm downright scared. But soon this is all going to be over. One way or another."

He gave a sharp nod. She was right. Bear Stevens would probably lie low for a while. Then, if he was, in fact, associated with Allison's stalker, he would make his way toward Cedar Key. He needed that sheet of paper. Someone had gone to a lot of trouble to get it. That someone hadn't given up. And neither would Bear.

Blake's jaw tightened. He needed to let Cedar Key PD in on what they had learned. All the agencies in the area would be alerted, but Bear had a direct connection to Allison. Sometime soon he would make his move. Blake had no doubt.

He only hoped they would be ready.

* * *

Allison stood at the helm, guiding *Tranquility* along its course paralleling the coast. A stiff sea breeze whistled past the sails and flattened the cloth brim of her hat against her forehead. Off the port bow, the last of the vibrant hues that stained the horizon were fading to navy. The seas were choppy, but her charter customers didn't seem to mind. They were probably too wrapped up in each other to notice.

She was right about them—honeymooners, spending their first week of life together in Cedar Key. The new bride was currently tucked under the young man's arm, snuggled against his side. She tilted her head up to smile at him, and he responded with a short kiss.

Allison sighed. These romantic sunset cruises used to send an acute sense of loneliness shooting through her. Actually, they still did. But now the loneliness was tempered with hope. For the first time since losing Tom, she was actually entertaining thoughts of something deeper than friendship.

She turned to glance behind her. As expected, Blake was holding his position about twenty yards off her stern, a distance which had gradually decreased as daylight faded to night. She was running a little late. But in another twenty minutes, she would be safely secured to the dock.

Up ahead, a green light flashed off the starboard bow, the beacon marking the entrance to the main shipping channel. On her nautical charts, it was simply called *flashing green four second*. For her, it marked the final stretch before home, the point at which she stopped paralleling the coast and pointed the bow toward Cedar Cove.

Her eyes widened as realization slammed into her. *Flashing green four second*, abbreviated Fl G4S. There was a G4 on the paper, too, but she had read the next symbol as a *5*. Was it really an *S?* And what about the R45? Was it supposed to be R4S, referring to a four-second red beacon? Then R2.55 was really R2.5S, a two-and-a-half-second red beacon.

Excitement surged through her, and her heart began to pound. Had she really cracked the code? All the hours studying the numbers, racking her brain, praying the mysterious characters would somehow make sense, and she figured the whole thing out without even thinking about it?

Well, not the whole thing. There were still the other numbers—87, 165 and 282. What did those represent? Measurements? Degrees on a compass?

She cast another glance at the Sea Ray in her wake. As soon as she could get rid of her charter customers, she and Blake would put their heads together and solve this thing.

The final leg from Seahorse Key to Cedar Cove seemed to stretch into forever. Finally, she eased up to the dock and tied off to one of the cleats there. Terrance sat on the deck of his boat, nursing a beer as he watched her work. The moment she looked his way, he averted his eyes. What was his problem? He'd never been superfriendly, but lately he seemed really put out with her. Or put out with the world.

Moments later, Blake motored into a slip and tied off. By the time the young couple headed up the dock toward their car, he was making his way toward her, Brinks several feet in front of him, straining at the leash.

She knelt on the cockpit seat to greet the dog, then smiled up at Blake. He was frowning.

"It's dark. There's no *almost* to it. We need to get you back to Harbour Master as quickly as possible."

"Not yet. I have something to show you."

His frown deepened. "Can't it wait till morning?"

"*It* can, but *I* can't." She lowered her voice to a hoarse whisper. "I think I might have figured it out."

Some of her own excitement seemed to rub off on Blake. But his was underscored with worry. "Why don't we discuss it in your room?"

"I need my nautical charts." She had a Raymarine chart plotter at the helm. But she would do this the old-fashioned way—with a paper chart, a pencil and a parallel ruler.

He hesitated a moment longer, then stepped onto her boat. Once below, she pulled a chart book and spiral-bound notebook from a shelf above the nav station.

Blake followed her to the dining area. "I thought we already decided the numbers couldn't be coordinates."

She laid the chart and tools on the table and slid to the back of the U-shaped bench. "They're not coordinates—at least not latitude and longitude." She picked up the pencil and scrawled some symbols on a sheet of paper she had torn from the spiral notebook. "Read this."

"R45 87, G45 165, R2.55 282." He looked up from the page. "It doesn't make any more sense than it did the last time I looked at it."

"You're reading it wrong. We've all been reading it wrong. These fives are *S*s."

Blake's gaze dropped back to the page. Finally, he frowned. "I still don't see it."

She slid the chart in front of him and pointed at one red elongated teardrop shape, then another and another.

His eyes widened. "Red four second, green four second and red two and a half second. They're beacon designations."

"And I'm thinking the other numbers are degrees on a compass. If we go 87 degrees from all the red four-second beacons, 165 degrees from the green four-second beacons, and 282 degrees from the red two-and-a-half-second beacons, I'm guessing there's going to be one point where three lines cross over an island. Or maybe the degrees are the directions the beacons are from the island, rather than the other way around."

As she talked, she laid the parallel ruler over the compass rose on the bottom of the chart and turned it until it crossed the 165-degree line. Once she had the other portion positioned over the beacon near Atsena Otie, she penciled a dark line. She did the same with every beacon in the vicinity of Cedar Key. There were over a dozen, lining both the main shipping channel and the Northwest Channel, along with a couple of outlying ones. She carefully measured out the appropriate degrees, until haphazard lines crisscrossed the chart. But there was only one point where three lines intersected—a spoil area along the Northwest Channel.

Blake pointed to the chart. "Bingo."

"X marks the spot. There's something there that Bear Stevens wants really bad."

"Bad enough to have someone ransack your house, put a knife to your throat and set your porch on fire."

His words doused a bit of the excitement she was feeling, reminding her of the danger she was in, even more imminent now that Bear was free.

"We need backup."

Before the words were out of her mouth, Blake was reaching for his phone. He scrolled through his contacts, looking for Hunter no doubt. The two of them had become close in recent weeks.

He put the phone to his ear and waited a span of two or three rings.

"Allison figured it out." He wouldn't need to preface the conversation with unnecessary details. Hunter had been involved from the start. "We don't know *what* he's after, but we know *where*."

After a brief pause, warmth filled his eyes,

along with approval and maybe even a little pride. "Yeah, she's a smart lady."

Her heart swelled. What he thought of her mattered. A lot.

"We want to head out first thing in the morning. Bear Stevens is out, and he's probably on his way here, even as we speak. So we'll need backup, whoever's on duty, as many as you can spare."

Within a few minutes, arrangements had been made, and Blake dropped the phone into his shirt pocket. "He's getting a hold of Chief Sandlin right now."

"Good." She slid to the edge of the bench and stood, suddenly anxious to be back in the safety of her room at Harbour Master Suites. If her intruder had any idea she had solved the code, she wouldn't even make it back.

Blake stood, too, but instead of heading through the galley and up the companionway steps, he slid both arms around her waist and pulled her close.

"You know what this means. In a few more hours, this will all be over. You'll have your life back."

A weight lifted from her shoulders, a burden that had been such a constant companion over the past few weeks, she had forgotten what it felt like to be free.

She wrapped her arms around his neck. "It's a good feeling. Although I have to admit, it's been kind of nice having you as my personal bodyguard."

"It's been nice *being* your personal bodyguard. But now that my job is coming to an end, there goes my excuse to keep hanging around." He was joking, but there was uncertainty behind the words.

And though she had tried not to think about it, she had had the same thoughts. While he was so wrapped up in trying to solve the case and see to her safety, there had been no time to think about the life he had left behind.

"If you need an excuse, I could probably come up with one. Or I could just tell you an excuse isn't necessary." She searched his eyes. "At least on my end."

His arms around her tightened. "When it comes to staying in Cedar Key, I have all the excuse I need, standing right here. I left

Dallas looking for direction in my life, some way out of the funk I had been in for the past eighteen months. The last thing I expected to do was fall in love."

Her heart began to pound. Blake was staying. For good. And he was staying because he loved her. And she loved him. It was futile to fight it.

Before she could voice all she was feeling, Brinks began to paw at her with the same urgency she had felt then forgotten the moment Blake pulled her into his arms. She laughed, then dropped an arm from Blake's neck to pet the dog.

"I think he's jealous. Either that, or he's reminding us we really need to go."

"Smart dog. We really *do* need to get you back to Harbour Master."

She swept up the chart book and clutched it to her chest. "I'm taking this with me. And this, too, unless you have one." She picked up her compass.

"Not a handheld."

She headed toward the companionway steps, then turned to face Blake. "On second thought, you should keep everything with you. It'll be safer that way."

Blake took the charts and compass and handed her Brinks's leash. Always eager for a walk, Brinks was the first one on deck. He immediately stood at attention, a low growl rumbling in his throat.

Allison froze halfway up. A figure stood on the dock, right next to her boat. Panic shot up her spine, then instantly dissipated. It was only Terrance.

She stepped into the cockpit, Blake right behind her. But a touch of uneasiness lingered. Something was wrong. That ultracool, beach bum persona that he always emitted was gone. Instead, he stood straight and stiff, weight equally distributed between both feet. And he didn't have his beer. Terrance never hung out around the docks without a beer in his hand.

Alarms went off in Allison's head. The only way off the boat was the dock where Terrance stood. She spun to face Blake, silently seeking direction.

Blake obviously felt it, too. His eyes were

narrowed, his posture stiff. "Hello, Terrance. What can we do for you?"

"Step onto the dock nice and easy." Terrance's words sent tendrils of unease sliding through her. The tough-guy timbre was there. But so was something else—an icy hardness.

She turned to face him.

And looked straight into the barrel of a pistol.

TWELVE

Brinks's low growl erupted into frenzied barking, and he lunged toward the dock. The leash stopped him two feet shy of sinking his razor-sharp teeth into Terrance's leg.

Terrance took a step back. "Tie up the dog if you don't want a bullet through his head."

Allison dropped to her knees and, with shaking fingers, began tying the end of Brinks's leash to a cleat. While she worked, Blake's mind whirled. Terrance was the intruder? The one who had been terrorizing her for the past four weeks? The idea just didn't compute.

Then again, maybe it did. According to Allison, Terrance had always come across as surly and rough, with a bit of a chip on his shoulder. But over the past month, that chip had grown, and he had gotten increasingly more moody.

And it was no wonder. For four weeks, he had been trying to get his hands on that paper. He had ransacked Allison's house, searched her boat, put a knife to her throat and set her house on fire to force her to give him what he wanted. And he had been thwarted at every turn. With each obstacle, his anger had built, not into a blinding rage, but a cold fury, which was much more dangerous.

So how did Bear Stevens fit into all this? Or did he? Was the timing of his prison break simply coincidence?

Allison straightened, and Terrance aimed the gun at Brinks, who hadn't stopped barking since they stepped into the cockpit. "Shut him up, or I'll shoot him."

"Brinks, sit." When the dog complied with the command, Blake gave a second. "Lie down."

Brinks hesitated, his ears back and a low growl rumbling in his throat. Blake gave the command again, and the dog finally obeyed, flattening himself against the floor of the cockpit. But he wasn't relaxed. Every muscle beneath that slick black coat rippled with tension.

Terrance repeated his earlier instructions. "Now get off the boat."

Allison held both hands up in front of her. "Terrance, think about what you're doing. You have a life here. Is whatever's out there worth giving that up to live a life on the run?"

"Quiet!"

Allison flinched at the sharp command, and Terrance continued.

"You call this a life? Working for you uppity people with your big boats and fancy houses? It's a great life for you, maybe, but not for the people who do your dirty work."

Allison's jaw dropped at Terrance's verbal attack, and Blake's stomach clenched at the hatred behind the words. His hand moved to his side. Her Glock was holstered there, hidden by his windbreaker. Could he use it? Would he have the guts to actually pull the trigger?

Resolve surged through him, and he had

no doubt. If it came down to Allison's life or Terrance's, he wouldn't hesitate.

"If you try anything, she dies."

Terrance's words froze him in his tracks. He would have to wait for the perfect opportunity. With Terrance's weapon trained on Allison's chest, now wasn't the time.

He stepped from the boat and glanced around him. Everything was deserted. No one lingered about in the parking area or on the back balconies of any of the Cedar Cove condominiums. If anyone had heard Brinks's barking, they had ignored it. Blake sighed. They were on their own.

"Walk toward my boat, both of you. And no heroics if you want to live."

Blake followed Allison down the dock, chart and compass clutched to his chest. But before he could board the old Bayliner, Terrance stopped him.

"Wait right there. Are you armed?"

As expected, Terrance found and removed the Glock within moments, then worked his way down each of Blake's legs. Finally, he straightened.

Blake breathed a sigh of relief. Terrance didn't check his shirt pocket, so he still had his cell phone. Not that it would do him much good. With Terrance watching his every move, he wasn't likely to have the opportunity to use it.

Terrance nudged him forward with the barrel of the gun, prompting him to board. Allison was already seated on the side-facing bench, and he moved to sit next to her. But Terrance had other ideas.

"You're going to captain the boat, and she's going to tell you where to go." He handed Allison a small flashlight, then settled onto the seat in the back. "Any monkey business out of either of you and you'll both be feeding the fish."

Blake gave Allison the compass and laid the chart across her lap. When her eyes met his, they were filled with fear. He took her hand and gave it a squeeze, offering an assurance he didn't feel.

"Break it up."

Allison flinched again, and Blake fought back a sudden urge to deck Terrance. He released her hand and sank into the pilot's seat. As he began to motor away from the dock, hopelessness descended on him. He had promised to protect her. How was he supposed to do that alone on a deserted island with an angry armed man?

He motored past the tip of Cedar Key toward the channel, his mind churning. If he could dial Hunter, maybe he could relay their plight unbeknownst to Terrance.

He slipped the phone from his pocket and laid it on the seat between his legs, keeping his left hand on the wheel. Without fully turning his head, he cast a sideways glance at Allison. She sat watching him, eyes alert. He swiped his thumb across the screen to unlock it and touched the icon to pull up his call log.

When he cast another glance at Allison, she was studying the chart in the glow of the flashlight Terrance had given her. She looked past the bow and held up an index finger. "Head toward the four-second red beacon."

"Will do." He cast the words over his shoulder so Terrance would hear. As long as Terrance was convinced they weren't trying anything, he would probably stay seated. If he stood and approached him from behind, Allison would find a way to warn him.

He glanced down at the phone, careful not to dip his head, and redialed his last contact. *Come on, Hunter. Pick it up. And listen carefully to what I'm going to say.* He slipped the phone back into his pocket and, confident the windbreaker would hide the glow, turned in his seat.

"Terrance," he began, "when Allison told you what was on that paper, she wasn't lying." He dipped his chin, bringing his mouth closer to the phone. "She thought the *S*s were *5*s. She just figured it out today, that those first designations are beacons and the other numbers are degrees on a compass." He repeated each line, then gave the final clue. "Once she drew the lines, they all converged on one of the Northwest Channel spoil areas."

"Whatever. Just drive."

Blake released a pent-up breath, trying to dispel some of the tension. He had done everything he could. There was nothing to do now but wait and hope for Hunter's help.

No, there was one more thing. He should have thought of it sooner. He had always handled things on his own, but now he was out of ideas.

He turned his thoughts heavenward and began to pray.

Allison pulled her windbreaker more tightly around her. Now that the sun had fully set, there was a chill in the early November air. But it didn't begin to match the cold knot of fear that had settled in her gut.

All the precautions they had taken were for nothing. Because here she was, speeding into the night, bouncing over the waves with a gun pointed at her head.

Was Terrance really capable of murder? The thought seemed almost inconceivable. But before tonight, she would never have imagined him being capable of any of the other things he had done, either.

And once he had what he sought, what would he do then? Would he leave them on the island to be rescued once daylight came? Or would he make sure he left behind no witnesses?

Or would he even have a choice? If he was working with Bear Stevens, Bear was likely calling the shots. A giant fist clamped down on her chest and squeezed.

But Blake had a plan. He had called someone. She was sure of it, even though she hadn't watched him do it. Not wanting to alert Terrance, she had averted her gaze shortly after he removed the phone from his pocket.

She clicked on the flashlight and shined it over the port bow. A shape appeared, a mini island created during dredging. It was the first of several spoil areas on the east-west stretch of the channel. A four-second red beacon flashed just ahead, a four-second green in the distance. If her calculations were right, their destination was between. Maybe they would be seen by some late-returning boater. The chances weren't good, but she was clinging to whatever hope she could find.

As they motored past the red beacon and

drew closer to the green, she once again shined the light over the port bow. "This is it."

The roar of the motor lowered in volume and pitch, and their forward movement slowed.

"Move around to the back side." The command was for Blake, but Terrance's eyes remained on her. So did the pistol.

As Blake circled around behind the small island, she tried to beat back discouragement. Terrance was lessening the chances of being seen, squashing what little hope she had. His boat would be out of sight. And though sparse, the scrub oaks and pines that had grown up would help hide them, too.

"Ease the boat to shore."

Blake did as told, cutting their speed even further. Finally, the *shhh* of fiberglass passing over sandy bottom whispered through the hull.

Terrance waved the gun at Blake. "Step ashore and set the front anchor."

Blake climbed onto the bow and eased himself over the rail, landing with a splash in the shallow water. Terrance's boat was pretty basic, no electric windlass or any other bells and whistles, so everything had to be done by hand. He measured out about twenty feet of rode and tied the line off to the front cleat. After unhooking the anchor from its brackets on the front rail, he carried it several yards inland and drove its pointed steel ends into the sand.

They were headed toward high tide, so there was no chance of the boat being grounded when they finished. Terrance would be able to board and take off…once he dealt with her and Blake. A shudder shook her shoulders.

"Okay." Terrance leaned forward to reach between the pilot's seat and the side of the boat. "Come back and get the shovel."

Shovel? Who carried a shovel on a boat? Allison turned to watch him lift the item from the floor and lay it on the bow. He was prepared and probably had been for a while, confident that it was just a matter of time until he got what he wanted.

And why not? No one suspected him. He was right there as she went in and out of the marina, even followed her on her charters a couple of times to ensure that she was safe.

She stifled a snort, kicking herself for once again being duped. It was the story of her life. When was she finally going to start looking behind the obvious? But somewhere beneath the silent castigation was the knowledge that she wasn't the only one who hadn't seen what Terrance was.

Once Blake had the shovel, Terrance took the flashlight from her, then gripped her arm and pulled her up. "Let's go. Leave the chart, but bring the compass."

She stuffed it into the pocket of her shorts, then scrambled forward, constantly aware of the pistol pointed at her back. By the time she reached the bow, Blake had dropped the shovel and stepped back into the dark, rolling water.

With her hands on his shoulders, she lowered herself into his waiting arms, and he carried her ashore. When he set her on her feet, he didn't release her right away. And for several brief moments, she reveled in the warmth of his embrace and the security she felt there.

Emotion welled up inside, and regret that she had never been able to express it.

"I love you." She wanted him to know. Chances were good neither of them would make it off the island alive.

His arms tightened around her, and he pressed his cheek to hers, his mouth close to her ear. "Stay alert. Don't give up."

Her breath caught, and her stomach rolled over. He *did* have a plan. She tilted her head back to meet his eyes.

"Get a move on. Now!"

Blake tensed, and she did, too. The steely voice was like a bucket of ice water thrown over her head, dousing that flicker of renewed hope. She pushed herself from Blake's embrace.

"Pick up the shovel and move away from the boat."

Terrance stood on the bow, the weapon pointed at both of them, careful not to get within strike range of the shovel. He was being cautious, and for good reason—he was outnumbered two to one. Of course, that lethal piece of metal he held had a way of evening things up.

She stepped back with Blake, then watched Terrance jump from the boat. He nodded at her and made a small motion with the gun.

"You're going to find the exact spot, and he's going to dig."

She gave a sharp dip of her head and swallowed hard, then walked in a tight, slow circle. All three beacons were visible from the island, casting their beams of light through the darkness. She chose the nearest one, the four-second red, and held up the compass. Her hand shook, making it hard to get an accurate bearing. Drawing in a steadying breath, she cupped her clenched fist with her other hand. It helped. But when she aligned the front and rear sights, she was a couple of degrees off. She needed to move left.

She dropped her arm and began walking toward the center of the small island, stopping to take regular bearings. Finally the number she sought lined up perfectly. One done, two to go. And adjustments to make on the first and second while she sought to line up the third.

Finally, she stopped and turned to face Terrance. She could no longer see the third beacon, the four-second green that marked the beginning of the main shipping channel. A small pine blocked her view, apparently having grown up since whatever they were seeking was buried. But she knew which direction it lay and was confident she had located the designated spot.

"This is it."

She looked from Terrance to Blake. The three of them stood in a loose triangle, Terrance still keeping his distance.

"Start digging." Terrance leaned back against one of the trees, but he didn't relax his stance or lower the weapon.

Blake stepped forward, drove the shovel into the ground and lifted a small mound of sand. Over the next ten minutes, an ever-widening hole appeared. Terrance grew more and more antsy, ratcheting her own tension up several degrees.

When Blake stopped digging and turned

to look at her, Terrance shoved himself away from the tree and strode toward her, fury flashing in his eyes. Fear exploded in her chest. What was he doing? She hadn't done anything to set him off. She threw up both hands and stumbled backward.

He reached around her to grab a handful of her hair and forced her to her knees. Blake started toward them, still holding the shovel. Then Terrance jammed the pistol into her temple. Panic pounded up her spine. *God, please help us.*

"You think this is one big game, don't you?"

Hand still fisted in her hair, he jerked her head backward. Pain shot through her scalp and neck, and a strangled scream made its way up her throat.

"You're stalling, trying to stretch it out. You keep looking at each other with those knowing glances, figuring I'm too stupid to know what you're thinking." His voice increased in pitch and volume, that cold control he had displayed all evening slipping. "Do you have any idea what you've put me through the past month? How many times

I've been called inept and incompetent, while you've gone on your merry way?"

Allison tried to still her spinning thoughts, to focus through the pain and fear. What was he talking about? Who had called him inept and incompetent? Surely not any of the residents of Cedar Key.

"You've stalled long enough. If you don't get moving and find this thing in ten minutes, I shoot her."

The panic she had been trying to hold at bay pounded up her spine and exploded through her mind. What if she was wrong? A miscalculation of one or two degrees could cause them to be off by several feet.

Blake resumed digging with renewed vigor, turning over large mounds of dirt. The hole expanded until it measured six-by-six by one foot deep and partially wrapped a small pine. He stopped digging and, holding the shovel vertical, drove it into the ground again and again. Finally, near the edge of the hole, his efforts met with a thud.

Relief washed through her. Once Blake finished uncovering whatever he had found, Terrance would probably still shoot them. But Blake had bought her some time.

Terrance suddenly released her. "Don't move."

He returned to the same tree he had stood by before and removed a cell phone from the case at his hip. After a few taps on the screen, he put the phone to his ear.

"We found it." A quick beat passed. "I don't know. I don't have it open yet. The girl's boyfriend is digging it up." There was another pause. Then Terrance's voice grew defensive. "Hey, I didn't have a choice. She had figured it out, and he was with her."

Allison watched him. Who was he talking to? Bear? Or someone else altogether? This someone was apparently calling the shots. And he wasn't pleased that Terrance had kidnapped both of them.

When she turned to look at Blake, he had stopped digging. He bent to lift the chest he had uncovered and placed it on the mound of sand.

Terrance took two steps toward him, then stopped. "Leave the shovel and go stand over there." He made a motion with the pistol, indicating a place about ten feet from where she knelt. "If either of you try anything, she's dead."

He closed the remaining distance, speaking into the phone. "It's uncovered. I'm getting ready to open it."

After stepping into the hole, he dropped to his knees. From her vantage point, he was in profile. He laid the phone next to the chest and briefly touched the screen. Had he disconnected the call? Her question was answered when a raspy voice shattered the silence.

"Well?" It was a single word, but managed to be impatient, demanding and condescending, all at the same time.

"I'm opening it now."

He placed the weapon within easy reach and pulled the flashlight from his pocket. Two latches held the lid closed. There was no lock. Whoever had buried it probably hadn't seen the need. It had apparently remained undisturbed for years.

Terrance unfastened the two latches and

slowly raised the top. In the beam of the light, the box appeared to be plastic with a rubber seal between the case and its lid, similar to the waterproof box that held her flares and flare gun. Except this one was larger. As he peered inside, she found herself holding her breath. What was inside the box? What was so important that it had cost her her serenity, her security, and probably her life?

Terrance's mouth fell open. Then he snapped it shut again to release a soft whistle. Finally, he reached in and pulled out a thick wad of bound bills, then another and another. Was he getting a cut? Was that what had enticed him to turn from honest work to a life of crime? It wouldn't surprise her. The promise of that kind of money could tempt a lot of people.

"Don't you be thinking of double-crossing me, boy." The harsh words seemed to jerk Terrance back to earth in a flash.

He began to stuff the bundles back into the box. "Just chill. I'm doing everything like we talked about."

"Good. Because if you double-cross me,

I'll come after you. There won't be anywhere on this planet you could hide that I wouldn't find you."

Terrance apparently chose to ignore the threat. "Everything has stayed dry. There doesn't seem to be a drop of water in here."

He removed a couple more bundles of cash from the container, then pulled something else from underneath—a sealed bag of white powder. Probably cocaine or heroin. He held it up in the beam of the flashlight. "What about the dope? You think it's still good?"

"It's pure, uncut. It's been kept cool and dry all this time, so it might be. How about we test that theory later."

Terrance smiled, pride straightening his spine. "That sounds like a plan. Am I picking you up where we talked about?"

Allison drew in a sharp breath as hope surged through her. Terrance was keeping his plans secret. Maybe he intended to let them live.

"Yep. I'm hiding out in an abandoned shed about a mile from the water. Text me when you get close." The voice on the phone fell silent for several moments. "Terrance? You know what you're going to have to do."

A sick sense of dread replaced the hope she had felt moments earlier.

Terrance rolled his shoulders, as if trying to dispel some tension. "I know. We already talked about it."

"You're not going to wimp out on me, are you?"

"Of course not."

"That's good, because Bear Stevens don't sire no wimps."

The words slammed into her, knocking the air from her lungs. They had been right about Bear Stevens all along. But they had missed one important detail. Terrance was his contact on the outside, the one doing all his dirty work.

Terrance was his son.

She'd never made the connection. No one had. Terrance grew up in nearby Chiefland with his mother. That was all anyone knew. He never spoke of his criminal father.

But that didn't mean he didn't talk to him.

Or want to win his admiration. Maybe even grow up to be like him.

She pulled her thoughts back to the conversation going on less than twenty feet away.

"This is your chance to make up for all your mess ups over the past month. You gotta be tough."

"I *am* tough. I'm gonna do this right. I'll make you proud."

He disconnected the call, picked up the weapon and stood. His intent was written all over his face. He stared at them, jaw set, eyes cold and devoid of emotion. "No loose ends."

Allison shook her head, trying hard to swallow the panic spiraling inside her. This was it. They were going to die. *God, please help us.*

She slowly rose to her feet. "You don't have to do this, Terrance. You don't have to follow in your father's footsteps. You can take us back to Cedar Key, and this will all be over."

Terrance raised the pistol. "You don't understand. I *do* have to do this. If I let you go, you'll go straight to the police. I'm not going to jail, and I'm not giving up this." He glanced at the plastic box beside him.

Blake took a single step forward. "Terrance, have you ever killed anyone before?" He took another step. "I have. And once it's done, you can't ever take it back." He took a third step. "Is that something you want to live with for the rest of your life?"

"Stop!" The word rang out clear and sharp. "My dad says I've always been a wimp. But I'm not. I can do what needs to be done."

He lifted the weapon, and Allison's heart stopped. He was going to shoot Blake. Then he would shoot her. And no one would know until some boater happened upon their bodies. All because she removed that stupid paper from the newel post and gave it to the police. It was one small decision, but it would cost her her life. And Blake's.

She sought his eyes, wanting to communicate everything she felt for him in the moments they had left. But his gaze was fixed on Terrance. Whoever Blake had called, whatever he had planned, it hadn't worked.

Terrance aimed. Squeezed his eyes shut. Drew in a deep breath.

And fired.

THIRTEEN

The instant Terrance closed his eyes, Blake flew into action. He sprang sideways, crumpled to the ground and did three sloppy somersaults. Pain shot through his knee, the worst he had experienced in months.

But he couldn't focus on that now. He grasped the shovel handle and sprang to his feet. But his bad leg buckled, twisting as he tumbled sideways. The pain intensified, a raging fire that nothing would quench. Stars filled his vision and blackness encroached. *Dear God, what have I done?*

Terrance opened his eyes and jerked the gun around. Only about seven feet separated them. But it may as well have been fifty. He would never be able to strike before Terrance took his second shot.

Then the low hum of an approaching powerboat drifted to them across the water. Terrance heard it, too, and his head swiveled in response.

Blake's breath came out in a rush. This was the break he had prayed for. He hoisted himself to his good knee and lunged forward, swinging the shovel with all his might. It connected solidly with Terrance's right hand. His weapon sailed through the air and landed in the sand ten feet from where Allison stood.

He shot her a glance. "Grab the gun!" His voice was strained as pain bore into his consciousness, threatening to shut everything else out.

Allison responded immediately. He had told her to stay alert, and she had. Before the words were all the way out of his mouth, she was diving for the weapon.

Terrance did, too, but she reached it first, rolled away and sprang to her feet. Respect and admiration swept through him, along with an undercurrent of envy. She executed the move exactly the way he had wanted to. But couldn't.

"Don't move." She stood with her feet

shoulder width apart, weapon aimed at Terrance's chest. "I'm not afraid to use this. You probably know that pink Glock you're holding on to is mine."

Terrance took a step back and raised both hands, his eyes never leaving Allison's face. She stood strong and poised, with all the confidence of a sharpshooter. But Blake knew better. She was bluffing.

"Bring me the weapon, sweetheart."

She hurried to him, and he took it from her before Terrance's mind registered the fact that it wasn't cocked.

He pulled back the hammer, and Terrance tensed.

"Hands behind your head. Now on your knees."

Terrance did as he was told, and Blake looked down the channel. A boat approached from the direction of Cedar Key. The hum grew louder, and dual spotlights appeared in the distance.

Allison dropped to her knees beside him. "You're hurt."

"I'll be all right." Maybe someday. He wasn't

kidding himself. This was no minor sprain. But he would deal with it later. Terrance was still armed.

"Remove Allison's Glock from your jacket. Slowly. Any sudden moves, and you're dead."

Again, he complied, holding it between a thumb and forefinger, barrel facing down.

"Now toss it over there."

When he did, Allison hurried to retrieve it, then returned to him with a frown, distaste settling in her features. One lesson at the shooting range hadn't changed anything. She was still not fond of guns, which made her display of bravery a few minutes ago that much more impressive.

Another sound joined the hum, this one more pulsing, and a spotlight circled the area. Hunter had done well. Not only was a boat speeding their way, but he had managed to get a Levy County sheriff's chopper in the air.

He cast a glance at Allison. "Get out in the open. Make sure they see you."

She hurried to the water's edge and looked up. The beam swept past her, then returned, bathing her in white light. The beacon coordinates had put them closer to the channel side of the island, and that was where she stood, waving her arms. She looked up the channel and flagged down the boat as it approached.

A minute or so later, it decelerated and nosed up to shore—the Cedar Key Fire rescue boat. The telltale fiberglass rails rising in a tall arc on each side gave it away. Bobby stepped off and made a beeline for Terrance, removing the handcuffs from his belt as he went. He was dressed in his Cedar Key Police uniform. His radio crackled, and he advised dispatch that everything was under control. Moments later, the chopper turned and headed back toward the mainland.

Blake held up a hand. "Before you let them go, we've got a lead on where Bear Stevens is hiding." The words came out strained. Blackness encroached further, and a hollow ring filled his head.

Bobby snapped the cuffs on Terrance's wrists. "Where?"

"An abandoned shed about a mile from the water."

"Abandoned shed where?"

The ring grew louder, and Blake lay back, panting. "They didn't say. Somewhere nearby, I'd guess. Terrance was supposed to get the loot and pick him up."

Bobby spoke into his radio, relaying the information to dispatch, and Blake let his head roll to the side. Allison was hurrying toward him, followed by Wade and Joe with first-aid supplies. Hopefully that kit Joe carried contained something for pain.

He closed his eyes, willing himself to remain conscious. Wade and Joe would get him temporarily patched up. Then would come the trip to the hospital for tests and possibly more surgery. Dread filled him as his mind flashed back to those agonizing months of recovery.

Here he was, at the beginning of another long, painful road. More time of inactivity followed by grueling physical therapy.

And he would do it in Dallas.

Now it was clear—he could no longer

stay in Cedar Key, entertaining unrealistic thoughts of a future with Allison. She was physically perfect. At one time, he was, too. But he had to face the facts. He would never again be what he once was—strong, active, athletic…a whole man.

Allison might be willing to spend the rest of her life tied to a cripple, but he couldn't do it. She would be hurt at first. But eventually she would move on. And she would find that perfect man—someone who was her match in every way.

Wade dropped to his knees next him. "Allison said you hurt your leg."

"Yeah, I avoided a bullet but blew out my knee."

"How bad is it?"

He tried to sit up, and a wave of nausea assaulted him. He stifled a groan. "It's bad. I don't know what I did, but when I tried to stand, it gave way and bent in a direction knees aren't supposed to bend."

Wade grimaced in sympathy. "Then we're going to go ahead and splint it right here and carry you to the boat. We'll have an ambulance waiting." Joe knelt on his other side and began laying out supplies while Wade continued. "Any other injuries? You're both okay other than that?"

Blake nodded. "Other than my knee, we're both fine. Thank God." He smiled up at Allison. "And yes, I have, several times." In fact, he hadn't stopped thanking Him since the moment the rescue boat appeared.

Bobby walked toward them, leading a cuffed Terrance. The toughness had ratcheted down several notches now that he was looking at jail time for kidnapping and possibly attempted murder. His head was bowed, his shoulders slumped. But he was too proud to offer excuses or plead for leniency.

Bobby smiled down at Blake. "Thanks for already having my job done. Good going, Detective."

"I can't take all the credit. Allison had a big hand in it."

She dropped to her knees and draped an arm across his shoulders. "You're the one who clobbered him with the shovel."

"And you're the one who got the gun. If not for that, we'd both be dead."

"I guess we make a good team."

The smile that lit her eyes should have warmed him from the inside out. Instead, it made his gut burn with guilt. The last thing he had wanted to do was hurt her. But he was left with no choice. To stay would be selfish.

"Hunter's on his way." Bobby tilted his head toward the water. The red glow of a port bow light moved down the channel. "I figured I'd catch a ride on the rescue boat. I knew this baby would get me here in a hurry."

By the time Hunter arrived, Wade and Joe had splinted his leg and were loading him onto the boat. Hunter stepped ashore, his gaze sweeping all of them. "Looks like I'm late to the party." His eyes settled on Blake. "Your call went to my voice mail. Fortunately I picked it up about fifteen minutes later. I thought you had pocket dialed me. But it didn't take me long to figure out you were in trouble and trying to give me clues." He frowned. "I would ask if you guys are okay, but it looks like you're not."

Blake looked up at him from the floor of the rescue boat. He sat propped up against the side, legs stretched across the back. A bead of perspiration made a track from his brow down the side of his face. But the blackness had retreated. Stabilizing his knee had helped. "Hey, we're alive. That's what counts. Several times tonight, I didn't hold out much hope."

Hunter shook his head. "I can't believe Terrance was behind all this. When you used his name on the phone, I thought I had heard wrong."

Bobby stepped up. He had sat Terrance on the sand nearby, waiting for a ride to shore. "It wasn't just Terrance. Bear Stevens masterminded the whole thing."

Hunter raised his brows. "Bear Stevens? What connection does he have with Terrance?"

"Father." It was Allison who answered the question.

Both Bobby's and Hunter's jaws dropped, but it was Hunter who found the words. "Bear is Terrance's father? I didn't see that coming."

"None of us did."

Bobby turned to Hunter. "Since we've got a kidnapping and an attempted murder, with a shot fired, I figured we'd let Levy County's CSI guys investigate. I'll go ahead and get everything I can from Allison, but we'd better wait till later to interview this one." He cast a glance at Blake. "He's not looking too great."

Blake gave them a weak smile. He wasn't *feeling* too great, either.

Hunter frowned. "The sooner we get him some help, the better. What about Terrance?"

"I've already read him his rights. I'll question him while I'm waiting for CSI to get here. Then I'll bring both him and his boat back. I'll have you follow us, just in case he tries something. And we'll have Allison ride with you. If I know her, she's going to be chomping at the bit to go be with Blake."

Blake slumped, that same guilt burning a path through the regret that already clogged his chest. Yes, Allison would stay by his side, compassionate and attentive. Those were two of the qualities that made her so special—two among too many to name. She was beautiful, inside and out.

And that was why he had to leave. If he stayed, she would probably look no further.

And she deserved so much better.

Water drained from the kitchen sink, leaving a min mountain range of white suds. Allison leaned against the counter and lifted her gaze to the window. Outside, the moon reflected off the Gulf in a shimmering white streak, moving with the gently rolling waves. The serene scene seemed to heighten her sense of melancholy.

Blake wasn't at his boat when she got in from her charter. When she had tried to call him, his phone went straight to voice mail. Had it gone dead? Or was he avoiding her?

Her chest tightened. For the past three days, he had seemed distant. Ever since getting hurt. Maybe it was the pain. Or the medications. But no matter how she tried to rationalize it, she couldn't shake the feeling that she was losing him.

Or maybe she never had him.

He had hinted at staying. But she had seen his restlessness, the frustration he felt with no longer being able to live on the edge. And she had seen how invigorated he had been once there was a bad guy to catch and a woman to protect. Now that the danger was over, would he hang around? Or would he be off in search of the next adventure? Was there anything to tie him to Cedar Key?

Was there anything to tie him to her?

The ring of the doorbell jarred her from her thoughts. She tensed, then forced herself to relax. Terrance was in custody. So was Bear—Chief Sandlin had gotten notification a few hours after they left the island.

When she looked out her living room window, her stomach rolled over. Blake and Brinks waited on her porch. She opened the door, and Brinks looked up at her, tail nub wagging and excitement rippling through him. Blake stood next to him, leaning on a cane, a brace on his right leg. Pain had etched lines into his features, lines that had been there for the past three days.

She swung the door wider, then backed up

to allow him entry. "You didn't walk here, did you?"

He stepped into the foyer. "I started to, but Bobby drove by and had pity on me."

She led him into the living room and, once he was seated, settled onto the couch next to him. Brinks sat in front of her and rested his head in her lap.

"I tried to call you after my charter."

"My phone was off."

No explanation, no apology. Her chest tightened.

Blake's eyes dipped to the floor then met hers. They held pain, but this pain wasn't physical. Dread pressed down on her.

"I came by to let you know I'll be leaving in the morning."

She swallowed past the lump in her throat and nodded, not trusting herself to speak. Hot tears tried to push their way to the surface, and she beat them back. She wouldn't cry. She had known from the start that his stay was temporary.

"I need to go back to Dallas. My doctors are there, my therapists." He gave her a half smile, but it was forced. "My time here has been great. And I have you to thank for that. But I can't stay in limbo forever."

She smiled, too, and hers was as forced as his. "You don't have to stay in limbo. People do settle down here, you know."

"I know, but it's time for me to go back." His gaze drifted until snagged by some invisible spot on the far wall. He drew in a deep breath, but instead of meeting her eyes, he frowned down at Brinks. "I don't know what to do with him. He mopes around all night long. I think he misses staying here."

Her gaze followed his to the big black head still resting in her lap. Brinks's dark eyes held sadness, maybe even pleading. Another wave of tears surged forward, and she shored up her defenses, trying to hold off the flood that threatened. Two droplets escaped anyway, trailing twin paths downward. The dam was weakening.

Blake repositioned himself on the sofa to turn toward her. He cupped her face and brushed his thumb across her cheek, smearing the moisture there.

"I'm so sorry. I never wanted to hurt you. But it's best that I go."

"Why?" She wasn't going to beg him to stay. But she wouldn't let him walk away without an explanation.

"Because if I don't leave Cedar Key, I won't be able to stay away from you."

"What if I don't want you to stay away?"

He pushed himself to his feet and stood facing her, leaning on his cane. "Look at me, Allison."

Her gaze swept over him, and the love that swelled in her heart sent pain shooting through her chest. Love wasn't supposed to hurt. But too often, it did. She stood and put both hands on his shoulders. "So you can't do everything you used to do. That doesn't matter to me."

"Maybe not now, but someday it will."

Anger flashed through the pain. "Who are you to say how I'm going to feel?"

"In this case, I'm more qualified than you are. Been there, done that." He spun on his good leg and limped toward the front door.

"I'm not your ex-fiancée!" She shouted the words at his retreating back.

He ignored her argument. "Come on, Brinks."

Instead of following, the dog pressed himself against her leg.

Blake called him again, with no more success than the first time. When he reached the foyer, he looked back at Brinks and heaved a sigh. "He loves me, but he adores you. If I take him, he's going to be miserable."

Her eyes sought out his. "You're thinking about leaving him here?"

"He would be happier. But only if you want him."

Brinks squeezed even closer, as if he understood the discussion and was making his choice known. She reached down to pet him. She had gotten attached to him over the past few weeks. But so had Blake. She could see it in his eyes. If she kept Brinks, Blake would be alone.

She squared her shoulders. He was the one who was choosing to leave, not her. And Brinks wanted to stay. She could make it work. A neighbor could take him out if she was tied up on a charter. Besides, as long as she had Blake's dog, there was that small sliver of hope that he might come back.

"He can stay."

Blake gave the briefest nod and opened the front door. Then he hesitated, jaw tight. Tension rolled off him, proof of the battle going on inside.

She rested a hand on his forearm. "Is this what you really want?"

He pulled away and stepped onto the porch. "No, it's not what I want. But it's best."

"What about what I want? Doesn't that matter?"

"What you think you want right now won't last. I don't want to be here the day you realize you made a mistake and want someone whole."

She shook her head, her heart twisting in her chest. "If you think I'm anything like her, you don't know me at all."

He opened his mouth, as if he had something else to say, then snapped it shut and turned away. Did he hurt as badly as she did? No. If he did, he wouldn't be leaving.

"I'm sorry, Allison." He spoke the words without turning around.

She watched him limp down the steps, make his way to the sidewalk and turn in the direction of Cedar Cove. She should offer to give him a ride back. But she couldn't. The dam was cracking, threatening to collapse. She was moments away from a total breakdown.

She stared several more moments at his retreating figure, knowing she would probably never see him again. Brinks let out a soft whimper and pressed his face against her hand. She drew in a shaky breath and backed into the foyer. The door closed with the softest thud.

And the dam broke.

FOURTEEN

Blake stepped gingerly around his boat, ready to cast off. Four days had passed since he'd trashed his knee. He had a bottle of pain pills, a cane and an official diagnosis—instability of ligaments due to damage. He also had a brace, something he would have to wear long-term, maybe indefinitely.

He released a sigh and let his gaze drift to the slip that *Tranquility* often occupied. It was empty. He knew it would be. Allison had a charter this morning. He was glad. Leaving would be easier.

Saying goodbye was the hardest thing he had ever done. Seeing the hurt in her eyes almost shredded his heart. But she was strong. In time, she would be all right.

He turned the key in the ignition, and the inboard hummed to life. When he rose to untie the dock line, Hunter was making his way toward him. He was out of uniform, apparently not on duty. He stopped next to the boat and crossed his arms.

"Where are you going?"

"Back to Dallas."

"That's what Allison tells me. Are you coming back?"

"Probably not."

"Why not?"

What, was he being interrogated? His annoyance came out in his tone. "Dallas is my home. My doctors are there."

"Uh-huh." Hunter wasn't buying it. Allison hadn't, either. "So how often are you having to see these doctors? Seems like the work's mostly done."

He shrugged. "I have to go through more physical therapy."

"And there aren't good physical therapists in Florida? I happen to have a friend who's an awesome physical therapist at Nature Coast Rehabilitation, right over in Chiefland."

"Well, good for your friend."

Regret nudged him before the words were

all the way out of his mouth. But everyone was beating him up. First it had been his mom. She had even gone so far as to tell him that she didn't want him coming back unless he had Allison with him. Now Hunter was here trying to keep him from leaving. Didn't anyone think he could manage his own affairs without interference?

He untied the first dock line and began to coil it, but before he could proceed further, Hunter stepped onto his boat. Indignation surged through him. No man stepped onto another man's boat without being invited.

"What are you doing?"

Hunter didn't respond, just moved to the console, turned the motor off and snatched the key from the ignition.

Blake asked the question again, with even more indignation than the first time. "What do you think you're doing?"

"Trying to keep two good friends from making the biggest mistake of their lives." He slipped the key into his pocket.

Blake took a step toward him, his stance threatening. "Unless you have a valid reason for detaining me, I'd suggest you give me back my keys."

"Not until you hear me out."

Short of challenging him to a physical duel, Blake was left with no choice. He crossed his arms and scowled at Hunter. "All right. Talk."

"I don't know Allison's entire past, but I know she's been hurt. And it's kept her from getting involved with anyone. Until now. She loves you, Blake."

"Look at me. I can't run, I can't do sports, I can't even walk without limping."

"Do you think she cares about that?"

"She deserves better than me."

"What she deserves is someone who'll cherish her. Someone who'll stay by her side and never leave her. Someone who loves her."

Yes, she deserved all of that. And more. More than he was able to give.

Hunter persisted. "Do you love her?"

"What I feel doesn't matter."

"Do you love her?"

"For someone like Allison, being tied to a cripple would get really old."

Hunter asked the question a third time, emphasizing each word, voice raised. "Do you love her?"

"Yes." His volume matched Hunter's. "Yes, I love her."

"Then I'd suggest you end your pity party right now and go fix things before you totally blow it."

Pity party? Was that what Hunter thought this was about?

Hunter pulled the key from his pocket and laid it on the seat. "Think about it. You've got a good woman who loves you just the way you are. Accept that. Don't make a decision you'll regret the rest of your life."

Then he stepped from the boat, walked up the dock and disappeared around the side of the Cedar Cove Beach and Yacht Club. And for several minutes, Blake just stood there, Hunter's words circling through his mind— *I'd suggest you end your pity party right now.*

Hunter didn't know what he was talking about. All his life, whatever had come his way, he had handled it. He had never felt sorry for himself.

Or had he?

Was he feeling sorry for himself now, and that was why he was pushing Allison away?

No. This wasn't about him. It was about her. Her life. Her future. Her happiness.

He stepped from the boat and began to pace, limping up and down the dock, the cane making little thuds against the weathered boards. In light of Hunter's wisdom, his arguments no longer sounded convincing.

No, it wasn't about Allison. It was all about him. He couldn't believe she would accept him, because he couldn't accept himself. She had freely offered him her heart. And he had thrown it back at her.

He spun on his good leg and limped to his boat, determination strengthening his steps.

Dear God, please help me fix the mess I've made.

Allison closed her eyes and drew in a clean, salt-scented breath, determined to lift her spirits. The sun was halfway through its ascent into a cloudless blue sky, and the temperature was a perfect seventy-five degrees.

It was another beautiful fall day. She was healthy, active and doing what she loved.

And she was alive. She had a lot to be thankful for.

She opened her eyes and let her gaze fall across her passengers—towheaded children in their little orange life jackets, two sitting with Dad and one with Mom. She had brought them out the main channel then had taken a northerly heading, past Seahorse and North Keys. Soon she would cross the Northwest Channel. That was the route Blake would take, headed back toward Texas.

Thank goodness she had a family today. If she had to deal with a couple of honeymooners all snuggled up making goo-goo eyes at each other, she'd burst into tears. Actually, she had shed so many last night that there probably weren't any left.

And after the tears had come the anger. He had broken down the walls around her heart, gained her trust and won her love. And all the while, he had no intention of staying. His talk about friends and family visiting them in Cedar Key had meant nothing.

She sucked in another deep breath, trying to expel Blake from her thoughts. But as she passed the mouth of the channel, she couldn't help glancing that direction. Had he left yet? Was he already well on his way?

A powerboat moved toward her, too far away to identify. At that distance, it could be anybody. She turned her attention ahead. After passing the channel, she took one look back. The boat had closed the gap, its speed more than double hers, even in the channel. And there was no doubt. It was Blake. She clenched her jaw and swallowed hard. Losing him was bad enough without having to watch him leave.

She turned her face forward, keeping her eyes on the horizon past the bow. A few minutes later, the distant roar of a motor rose over the sounds of the wind and waves. Probably Blake coming out of the channel. She wouldn't look. It would only make it worse.

The roar grew closer. Someone was overtaking her. That was likely to be Blake, too. He would turn north and follow the coast all the way to Texas. Why hadn't she sailed the other direction? She could have spared herself the grief altogether.

The roar grew louder until she could no longer ignore it. It sounded as if he was ready to climb over her transom. She turned in time to see him overtake her on the starboard side then cut back the throttle until he was doing little more than idling. He was matching her speed, their side rails less than ten feet apart. He also had the attention of her charter customers, adults and kids alike.

She glared at him. "Are you crazy? What are you doing?"

"We need to talk."

"Out here?"

"I couldn't wait until you got back. I love you, Allison."

She ignored the way her stomach flipped. "So you've said. But it's not stopping you from leaving."

"I'm staying in Cedar Key."

"What?" She had to have heard him wrong.

He spoke louder. "I'm not going back to Texas. I'm staying in Cedar Key."

She had heard him right the first time. He

was staying. All the possibilities tumbled through her mind. But only one word would form. "Why?"

"Because of you, sweetheart. I can't leave you. I want to spend the rest of my life with you."

Her mouth fell open. "Are you proposing to me?"

"What if I am?"

The oxygen seemed to flee her brain, leaving her giddy. "Proposing on a boat is romantic. Proposing from one boat to another is just weird."

"Then pull over."

"What do you mean, 'pull over'? This isn't a highway."

"Go back to Seahorse Key."

She heaved an exasperated sigh. "In case you haven't noticed, I'm on a charter. These people have paid good money for me to take them sailing."

The woman spoke up. "We'd love to go to Seahorse Key. We wanted to see the lighthouse and were disappointed we wouldn't be able to fit it in. This is our opportunity."

"Are you sure?"

"You need to talk with your man."

"But this is your charter. I can talk to him later."

The husband waved away her protest. "Don't argue with her. You won't win. She's a counselor. Saving relationships is her job. There's no way she's going to let this go."

She turned the wheel, and as the bow came around, her heart pounded with the knowledge that her whole life was about to change. Was she ready? She had thought she was. But now that the possibility of a marriage proposal was staring her in the face, she wasn't so sure.

All the way back to Seahorse Key, her mind whirled. By the time she anchored, she was more confused than ever. She brought her customers to shore in two trips, and the kids took off running the moment their feet hit solid ground. Seahorse Key had been a good choice.

After motoring back to pick up Blake, she pulled the dinghy onto the beach, and they set out walking, staying near the water's edge where the sand was more firmly packed. They moved slowly, Blake's cane making deep circular indentations. A gentle sea breeze blew across the island, and a half dozen hopeful seagulls waited on the sand a few yards ahead of them. In the distance, the top of the lighthouse rose over the trees. Yes, a walk on Seahorse Key had been an excellent choice.

"I thought for sure you'd be well on your way to Texas by now. What changed your mind?"

"A solid chewing out by Hunter."

Hunter? She wasn't sure whether to thank him or scold him for sticking his nose in her business.

Blake continued. "He gave me a good tongue-lashing, made me see some things that I was blind to before."

"Like?"

"Like how you're a special lady. And how big of a mistake I was making by walking away." He took her hand in his. "I'm not going to lie to you. I can't do the things I used to do. The way I am now, this is permanent. I don't want to hold you back."

She sighed in exasperation. "How is that going to hold me back? I'm not planning to take up mountain climbing. I sail, I go to church, I sing, I hang out around Cedar Key."

"I think I can handle all those activities." A slow smile climbed up his cheeks. "Except singing. But that has more to do with a lousy voice than a bad knee."

She laughed, a wonderful sense of contentment sweeping over her. Up ahead, her charter customers rounded up their brood and turned down the path leading to the lighthouse. If they wanted more sailing time, she could give it to them. They were her only charter for the day. The evening she would reserve for Blake. She had a feeling she would be reserving a lot of evenings for him.

She looked back up at him. "Now that you're staying, what are you going to do?" She couldn't imagine him being content with stocking shelves the rest of his life.

"Look for a teaching job. My first call will be the College of Central Florida. I did some checking before, and they offer a law enforcement officer basic recruit training class. But I don't know whether they offer it at the Chiefland campus."

"I hope that works out." It would be perfect for him, a way to use his police training without the physical demands.

"I'm also going to get my teaching certification for Florida. But if I teach kids, it'll have to be middle school and up. I'm not sure I'd know what to do with rug rats." He grinned, then again grew serious. "Unless they were my own."

He pulled her to a stop, laid the cane on the sand and took both of her hands in his. Her heart stuttered, and her stomach did a series of backflips. This was it. He was going to ask her to marry him. She didn't want to say no, but didn't know if she could say yes.

He looked down at her, his eyes filled with understanding. "I know you've been hurt. You've had your trust shattered. But I want to prove to you that you can trust me one hundred percent."

He shifted his position, his hands tightening during the brief moment when all his weight was on his right leg. "I can't do this the official way and get down on one knee, or I'd never get back up. But my request is just as humble and heartfelt. Allison, will you marry me?"

Before she could respond, he hurried to explain. "I don't need an answer right now. I'm willing to wait as long as it takes."

He continued to stare down at her, his gaze warm, his eyes pleading. And the last of the barriers came tumbling down. Love surged through her, so powerful it left her dizzy. If he could trust her with his heart, she could trust him with hers.

She pulled her hands free to wrap her arms around his neck. "Yes, I'd love to marry you."

Relief flashed across his features, then joy. Whatever came next, she couldn't say. Because in that moment, he covered her mouth with his own. Everything he felt was poured into that kiss.

And she responded with the same passion. What she shared with Blake was an unexpected and precious gift. For almost three years, she had hidden behind the walls of distrust, secure in the knowledge that no man and his secrets would ever again upend her life.

But Blake had broken through those walls with his love and honesty. And she lost herself in his kiss, sure that any remaining secrets were little ones.

* * * * *

Dear Reader,

I hope you've enjoyed your visit to Cedar Key. Several years ago, my husband and I were sailing in the Suwannee area and stopped at Cedar Cove Beach and Yacht Club to get gas, not knowing gas wasn't sold there. Right away, a gentleman loaded my husband and our portable gas tank onto his golf cart and took him across the island. During that short stop, we fell in love with the quaint setting, "Old Florida" atmosphere and friendly people. So when I decided to write a series of books set in an island community, Cedar Key had to be the place. Storms have destroyed the docks behind Cedar Cove since we initially sailed in, but the Cedar Cove Beach and Yacht Club is a real place, as are the other business establishments in the book.

I had fun writing Allison and Blake's story and hope you could relate to them. They had both been wounded by events in their pasts. Allison found healing and strength through a relationship with God but was still guarded. Blake continually kicked himself for mistakes in his past and couldn't accept Allison's love for him until he learned to accept himself.

I hope you'll return to Cedar Key for books two and three in the series, where first Hunter and then Darci each find their happily-ever-after.

God bless you.
Carol

Questions for Discussion

1. Although Allison found love and acceptance from those in her Cedar Key church, Blake felt Christianity was simply a bunch of dos and don'ts. Have you ever been part of a church that seemed to focus more on following the rules than God's grace? How can you reach someone who has experienced judgment rather than love from Christians?

2. Before Blake's injury, he had been extremely athletic. Afterward, he struggled with self-esteem issues and had a hard time believing that Allison could truly love him with his physical limitations. How can you help someone who is going through that kind of a life change? What words does God have regarding our worth to Him?

3. After learning she had been deceived by her deceased husband, Allison believed everyone has secrets and was afraid to

trust. Are you the type of person who naturally looks for the good in people you meet, or do you tend to be more suspicious? How do you interpret Matthew 10:16, "Be as wise as serpents but as harmless as doves"?

4. Terrance tried all his life to gain the love and respect of his father but never succeeded. This led him to make some bad choices. Do you know any young people who are headed down that path? What can we do to influence for good the youth in our lives?

5. Blake felt extreme guilt over his part in the death of a twelve-year-old boy. Although most people haven't accidentally killed someone, many carry regret over past mistakes. What are some ways to find freedom? What does the Bible say about guilt and God's forgiveness?

6. Allison's discovery of the paper in her newel post set up a chain of events that changed her life. Have you ever had one

decision or event make a significant impact on your life? Was it in a good or bad way?

7. Blake's partner betrayed him in the worst possible way. Betrayal stings, especially when coming from someone close. Have you ever been betrayed by a family member or close friend? What are some ways to move past the hurt? Knowing that God requires us to forgive those who wrong us, how can we release the resentment and act in love toward that person?

REQUEST YOUR FREE BOOKS!

2 FREE INSPIRATIONAL NOVELS IN TRUE LARGE PRINT

PLUS 2 FREE MYSTERY GIFTS

Love Inspired

TRUE LARGE PRINT

YES! Please send me 2 FREE Love Inspired® True Large Print novels and my 2 FREE mystery gifts (gifts are worth about $10). After receiving them, if I don't wish to receive any more books, I can return the shipping statement marked "cancel." If I don't cancel, I will receive 3 brand-new true large print novels every month and be billed just $7.99 per book in the U.S. or $9.99 per book in Canada. That's a savings of at least 20% off the cover price. It's quite a bargain! Shipping and handling is just 50¢ per book in the U.S. and 75¢ per book in Canada.* I understand that accepting the 2 free books and gifts places me under no obligation to buy anything. I can always return the shipment and cancel at any time. Even if I never buy another book, the two free books and gifts are mine to keep forever.

117/317 IDN F5FZ

Name	(PLEASE PRINT)	
Address		Apt. #
City	State/Prov.	Zip/Postal Code

Signature (if under 18, a parent or guardian must sign)

Mail to the **Harlequin® Reader Service:**
IN U.S.A.: P.O. Box 1867, Buffalo, NY 14240-1867
IN CANADA: P.O. Box 609, Fort Erie, Ontario L2A 5X3

* Terms and prices subject to change without notice. Prices do not include applicable taxes. Sales tax applicable in N.Y. Canadian residents will be charged applicable taxes. Offer not valid in Quebec. This offer is limited to one order per household. Not valid for current subscribers to Love Inspired True Large Print books. All orders subject to credit approval. Credit or debit balances in a customer's account(s) may be offset by any other outstanding balance owed by or to the customer. Please allow 4 to 6 weeks for delivery. Offer available while quantities last.

Your Privacy—The Harlequin® Reader Service is committed to protecting your privacy. Our Privacy Policy is available online at www.ReaderService.com or upon request from the Harlequin Reader Service.
We make a portion of our mailing list available to reputable third parties that offer products we believe may interest you. If you prefer that we not exchange your name with third parties, or if you wish to clarify or modify your communication preferences, please visit us at www.ReaderService.com/consumerchoice or write to us at Harlequin Reader Service Preference Service, P.O. Box 9062, Buffalo, NY 14269. Include your complete name and address.

ReaderService.com

Manage your account online!

- Review your order history
- Manage your payments
- Update your address

---

*We've designed
the Harlequin® Reader Service
website just for you.*

Enjoy all the features!

- Reader excerpts from any series
- Respond to mailings and special monthly offers
- Discover new series available to you
- Browse the Bonus Bucks catalogue
- Share your feedback

Visit us at:
ReaderService.com

RS13TR